Stuck in Love

THREE SEXY
FORCED PROXIMITY
NOVELLAS

JENNY BUNTING

Please Be Seated Editing: Jenn Lockwood Editing

In Case of Emergency, For Your Safety Editing: Lopt & Cropt Editing

Proofreading: Horus Proofreading

Cover Design: Elle Maxwell

For every person who ever let me out so I could go to the bathroom on a flight. You're the MVP of my life.

For the person who requested to smell my hair in the comments of one of my YouTube videos. I've never forgotten you.

To the middle schoolers we shared a water ride raft with at Six Flags a few years ago. In the immortal words of Lee Ann Womack, I hope you dance.

CONTENTS

BOOKS BY JENNY BUNTING

A NOTE FROM JENNY

Thank you for picking up *Stuck in Love: Three Sexy Forced Proximity Novellas.* I hope you enjoy them.

This is a bind-up of three previously published titles of mine: *Please Be Seated, In Case of Emergency,* and *For Your Safety.* These novellas have been lightly edited from the original editions but they're still the same great stories.

This edition also includes a bonus chapter at the end of each novella. It's told from the male love interest's point of view, when each heroine left his life for the last time.

These novellas include open door, explicit sex scenes and coarse language. Additionally, some of the couples get stuck in situations that might be distressing to some readers. Everybody gets out...promise!

Please
be
Seated

1

I will need at least two Bloody Marys.

No, make it three.

After meeting after meeting in a windowless boardroom in Manhattan, my body needs something, anything, to relax my residual stress. This airplane seat does nothing for the cause. I feel constricted, uncomfortable, and downright grouchy. The meeting ran late, resulting in me sprinting through the terminal at JFK like I was on *Supermarket Sweep* with no time to change into comfortable plane clothes. So, now I'm sitting here, wearing my stiff boardroom pantsuit, my curls flattening to a breath of a wave, and my makeup rubbing off in chunks.

I look at my carry-on purse longingly. It holds my favorite leggings and a baggy white T-shirt. My friend and roommate, Cassie, makes fun of me constantly for the baggy-shirt-and-leggings look—ever since it became my off-work uniform four months ago. It's comfortable, even if it hangs off of me now since I completely lost my appetite and am barely regaining the weight I lost. It looks sloppy, but in a chic way.

The guy to my left plasters himself against the plane wall while I scrunch into the middle seat. The aisle seat is empty, and I pray silently it stays that way. It's mine if no one occupies it. I fantasize about freely using the restroom, stretching my legs, and maybe changing in the airplane bathroom. The flight is semi-full—a red-eye from New York to San Francisco—and blissfully quiet. I hear faint rap music from my rowmate's headphones, but other than that, I can work with this. I may even be able to sleep.

Who am I kidding? I don't sleep on planes.

I just wonder when the drink cart service starts. I have five hours and several drink coupons for Skyline Airlines saved up for an emergency like this. I might pass out from too much alcohol accidentally—which is the best-case scenario.

It's better than being alone with my thoughts.

I pull out my phone to shoot off a text prior to forced airplane mode.

Me: About to take off. Pick me up at 1 am. Love you.

Cassie: You're lucky I love you. You are the only person I stay up that late for. Anyone else can take a Lyft.

Me: At least I'm not flying into Oakland.

Cassie: True.

I turn my phone to airplane mode and tuck it back into my carry-on.

Although she makes fun of my wardrobe, I do not deserve Cassie. She was there when everything went down with Patrick, and she let me move in to her four hundred square foot studio in the city when I moved out of his apartment in Berkeley. I snuck out today to buy her her favorite cupcakes from a New York exclusive bakery as a first of many thank-yous.

I bought myself two and thought I would eat them. Instead, they got added to Cassie's stash.

The aisle has emptied, and I rub my palms together. The aisle seat is mine. I unbuckle my seatbelt to move, since it appears safe. Just then, a man rushes onto the plane like he is going to propose to some unsuspecting girl.

That only happens in movies pre-9/11, but still, one can hope.

I need to believe in love again—even if it happens to someone else.

The flight attendant approaches him, and he flashes his phone. He is all smiles as he waves to other passengers, thanking them for their patience. The flight attendant leads him back, dangerously close to me and my rap-listening rowmate. I cringe as she stops at our row and presents the seat to him like it's an entrée at a Michelin-starred restaurant.

Fuck.

"Hi," he says to me. I respond with a closed-mouth smile. He opens the already-closed overhead bin to shove his carry-on in. The flight attendant assists him as well. The vitriol pouring out of the other passengers is potent as this carefree dude rearranges their items so his can fit last minute.

He sits down, bouncing with the force.

"I'm Landon," he says, holding out his hand. With great hesitation, I take it and shake. His hand is smooth, and his handshake is firm. He is wearing a comfortable plaid shirt over a gray T-shirt and jeans.

I am so jealous.

"I'm so glad I made it! Getting here was a nightmare. I don't have great time management, so this isn't the first airplane I've almost missed."

He smiles widely, his mouth full of impeccably white and straight teeth. He stares at me, and my head jerks. Why is he still looking at me?

"What's your name?" he asks.

"Oh, Erin," I say. "Erin Campbell."

"Oh, we're doing last names, too. Mine is Walcott. Landon Walcott." He smiles again, his teeth practically sparkling.

I scrunch myself further into my seat. Of course I am stuck next to the chatty, tardy guy on the plane.

I lean my head back. The drink cart cannot come soon enough.

I close my eyes, but my rowmate asks, "Why were you in New York?"

I open my eyes, and Landon is right there, smiling wide enough to show gums.

"My company is interested in acquiring another company, and I was there to grease the wheels."

"Oh, like in *Succession*? I love that show. Do you watch that show?"

"Yes, but..." I begin.

"I binged it a few weeks ago," Landon interrupts me. "Everyone is *awful*. I am obsessed, though. My roommate, Henry, and I binged that in a week and a half. Nonstop."

More smiles. He needs to pace himself, or his cheeks will be sore.

"I'm trying to get a promotion, so I volunteered," I offer. Rarely do I keep conversations going with strangers, but the longer I look at him, the cuter he becomes.

"I bet you're great at your job."

"I'm okay." He holds eye contact with me, and I squirm. Am I supposed to ask what he was doing in New York? Fine, I'll bite.

"What were you doing in New York?" I ask.

"Well, I had my own meeting," he says, straightening an imaginary tie. As I examine him closer, he is definitely good-looking. Bright-green eyes, a scruffy square jaw, and a lanky build. His sandy-blond hair screams *I have no problems, ever.*

"What do you do?" I bite again.

"I created a dating app. Well, my friend and I created a dating app. We thought of it when we were watching *Love is Blind* while we were high, and Henry is a coder, so…"

"I love that show," I say, snapping my fingers. I binged the entire first season in two days after Patrick and I ended our engagement. I cried during every episode.

"So, we created an app. Kindred. Have you heard of it?"

I nod. Practically all of my single friends are on it. I even created a profile for myself, but I haven't made it public yet. Kindred's premise is you choose matches based off of written profiles before you see pictures. I understand the thought behind it, but some of my friends have been ghosted the second pictures were exchanged.

"Anyway, someone wants to buy it. Henry gets really anxious, so I went. I am the more extroverted of the two of us," Landon says. He gives two thumbs up. Usually, I would find this nauseating. On Landon, it's downright endearing.

"Did you get an offer?" I ask. I don't know if I care or not; it's just nice talking to someone so upbeat.

"Yeah, but I don't know. It's our baby. I'm *so* proud of it. This app is special. My other apps are special, too, but…"

"You've created other apps?"

Landon nods confidently. "App creation is my passion."

I nod. My job is *not* a passion. Being part of a large corporation buying out smaller corporations is not noble work. I am above-average at my job; hence, why I get sent across the country instead of solely being a cubicle jockey. A promotion is being dangled in front of me. I'm not sure if I want it because I actually want it or because it's the next benchmark.

"You look uncomfortable," Landon says.

"I am," I reply. "I was late and didn't have a chance to change prior to boarding. If I would've known you were going to hold up the plane…"

"I know, I know," he says, holding up his hands.

Oh good, he can take a joke.

"Well, as soon as the *Fasten Your Seatbelt* sign is off, I will block all other passengers for you so you can change in that tiny bathroom. Awkwardly." He nudges me, and it feels like we're pals, even though we just met five minutes ago.

"As a thank you, I have all these Skyline drink coupons," I say, pulling out an accordion of gray and white vouchers. "You can help me drink watered-down alcohol."

"Excellent," Landon says, rubbing his hands together. "It is *so fun* to get drunk on planes."

"Exactly," I say with a smile. Wow, I'm smiling. Besides a smile in reaction to a cute dog story, it has been a while since I smiled at anything. Landon's positive energy is infectious, like a virus of joy. It makes me forget my crummy life for a second.

A flight attendant stations herself in the middle of the plane with an incomplete seatbelt. Landon and I watch the presentation, and Landon mimics the flight attendant, complete with hand gestures.

"I will put on your mask first," Landon says. "And then my mask."

"Not if I put yours on first," I joke. Landon's grin brightens, and I check myself. Am I grinning, too? I touch my cheeks, and I definitely am.

The plane starts moving, taxiing. I can see the guiding lights in the dark as our plane gets in line to take off.

"I may be thirty-one years old," Landon says. "But I still get nervous taking off."

I did not guess thirty-one. He bounces in his seat like a golden retriever puppy, all smiles and wags. I guess never having anything go wrong in your life keeps you youthful.

It could explain why I only see hag when I look in the mirror.

"Will you hold my hand?" Landon asks. "I get very, very, very scared."

He places his hand on the armrest, and I look down.

Why the hell not.

I connect my hand with his. My hand in a stranger's hand looks foreign...but comforting. He smiles, and I smile again.

The plane speeds down the runway, and Landon mouths "Woah" to me, his mouth a long O. Usually, I ignore the turbulence and settle into boredom on an airplane. Sometimes, I try to work—I never sleep—or I'll read the SkyMall magazine.

Holding the hand of a stranger who becomes more handsome by the smile is a delightful new development.

Once the plane reaches altitude, Landon disconnects hands and reaches for the pouch paper materials. Landon opens the drink menu dramatically. "It looks like cocktails or tiny bottles of wine are our options."

"It's hard to screw up a gin and tonic. Or a vodka and tonic. I'm craving a Bloody Mary myself."

"Bloody Marys are delicious. Should I chance the Island Margarita? To celebrate that Skyline now travels to Oahu?"

"It's probably orange juice and tequila."

"Ew, you're probably right," Landon says. He turns to me

with soft eyes. "I wasn't kidding. The minute that sign comes on, I will block anyone who tries to dash for the toilet before you."

"Thank you. I can be patient if someone is a nervous-bowel-movement person."

"I'm sure they'll appreciate it," Landon says.

It's nice to have someone to talk to, even for a little while. When I had Patrick, I ignored my compounding hatred for my job and mind-numbing rut of a routine. Now, I feel lost and unsure what to do. A reprieve from my thoughts, like Landon, is always welcome. This kind, good-looking man is a godsent distraction to my monotony. There is no way this will result in anything substantial or anything more than a light flirtation.

"What is that?" Landon asks, sniffing his nostrils.

I perk up, sniffing in the aroma as well. I definitely smell it. I cover my mouth and my nose to keep the putrid odor out.

"What is that?" I ask.

2

The smell grows stronger, and I cough in response. Other passengers' heads pop up like meerkats, investigating the odor as well. I stretch my body to look in other rows; I look to my right, but it's not that row. Everyone is asleep.

Landon grabs my forearm, and I feel warm all throughout, even if my nose is on fire.

"I will get to the bottom of this smell—when the seatbelt sign goes off." Landon points to the ceiling, and the seatbelt sign glows in its tyranny.

"Oh my *God*," a woman screeches, and I see the culprit.

A pair of hairy feet with yellow talons for toenails rest casually on an armrest. I see the smelly asshole's head who lounges without shame. I point around Landon, and he gasps.

"Someone has to tell him his feet are nasty," I whisper.

"Maybe he knows, and he doesn't care. My Uncle Harry is like that. Wait, is that my Uncle Harry?" Landon lifts slightly from his seat. "No, it's not him. Too much hair on the head."

"Do you think anyone is going to say anything?" I ask. I peer around the row, and now the toes are spread apart like fingers. Gross. There is whispering but no blatant signs of response.

"I doubt it. Though, you never know."

The smell loses its aggressive rottenness, and I can breathe without my eyes watering. The whispering dies down, and he finally takes his feet off the armrest. Now, I'm just excited to tell everyone about this shoeless guy, even if the ordeal lasted two seconds.

I also cannot wait to tell everyone about this really cute guy who made a ho-hum flight great.

A ding sounds from overhead, and we look up to see the seatbelt light is off.

"It's your moment to shine!" Landon says as he barrels out of the aisle and stands up, almost falling into an older woman asleep with her mouth open.

I grab my carry-on and brush past Landon. The quick swish of our clothes sends goosebumps up my arms. We share a smile, inches from each other's face, and he pats my upper back with his palm. More goosebumps.

"He's also eating a full bag of pork rinds," Landon whispers. The shoeless, unapologetic man grabs a fistful of the snack and crunches loudly. From the back, I see his rowmate squirm. I feel bad for her.

I charge the rear of the plane.

I half-smile at the flight attendant, still strapped in the jump seat, scrolling on her phone. The bathroom door sticks, and I brace my weight to push the door open. I have zero upper body strength so this is about to get comical, real fast. It finally opens with a *thwack,* I don't fall in, and relief washes over me. I'm so close to being comfortable I could cry. I also want to get back to my seat. To Landon.

I set my bag down on the toilet and immediately strip out of my jacket and pull my stiff blouse over my head.

Visions of Landon slowly undressing me come out of nowhere.

I've known Landon for thirty minutes, and I'm already having sexual fantasies about him. Great.

It has been a while since I've had sex. As the wedding with Patrick loomed, we slept together less and less. He did not reach for me, and I fell asleep in an exhausted heap every night. I thought not sleeping together for a month prior to our wedding was normal; we would rip each other's clothes off once the stress of the wedding was over. Patrick calling it off definitely affirmed that, no, we had a problem.

Somehow, we lost each other.

Landon is not a good fixation for my sexual fantasies. First off, we're on a plane. Joining the Mile High Club does not appeal to me, and I would never attempt it. With my luck, I would get stuck in the bathroom or fall out, buck naked. Second, I barely know him. I've only had sex with men I've dated, and who knows if Landon and I will see each other past this plane ride. Seeing someone's bare feet always leads to bonding, but I don't think enough to bump uglies.

I avoid the mirror as I stuff the suit in crumples and pull on my favorite leggings that feel like butter on my legs and my trusty black flats. I breathe out a sigh of relief. My hair is doing nothing for me, so I collect half of it into a bun on my head and find some blessed makeup wipes. As I remove the layers of professional makeup, my skin breathes, and I feel better. I check my appearance once last time. Maybe I'm checking it so I look good for Landon. Even if there's no chance for sex or romance in the immediate future, I still want to feel nice and pretty.

After I collect all my belongings and deposit my wipe in the trash, I try the door, and it doesn't budge. Huh. Even with more force, my yanks do nothing. Maybe setting my stuff down would help? I prop my bag on the closed toilet and turn around, bracing my feet to pull this mother-fucker open. I change arms in case that helps. Nope. I double-check that it's unlocked. It is. Why won't you open? I even stick my tongue out to harness magical door-opening capabilities.

Nothing.

Then, I do what any normal, sane woman would do. I start screaming and banging the door like a lunatic. Flashes of news stories about "Woman Stuck in Bathroom on Skyline Airlines Flight Has to Be Sedated" scroll through my mind. Would they have to land the plane?

"I'm coming—don't worry!" a female voice says from the other side. "Is it unlocked?"

"Yes!" I yell, still pulling.

"Okay, it'll be fine! I promise," she says calmly. "This has been sticking a lot lately."

It takes roughly twenty seconds of joint effort until I see my hero. The door finally dislodges, and she stands there. She has dark hair tied back in a classy bun and wears the navy-and-yellow uniform well.

"Oh wow, I thought I needed to get the jaws of life to get you out!" she jokes. I smile hesitantly, the claustrophobic trauma still buzzing through my veins. She continues with a hand flip. "That door has been sticking forever. I keep telling the higher-ups we need to fix it, but they never listen to me. At least one person gets stuck every flight."

I wonder about the liability, but the flight attendant says in a hushed tone, "Do you want something to drink? I can get it for you before everyone else."

She taps into one way to get me to forget any stressful situation. Alcohol. I remember the Island Margarita, the drink Landon had his eye on. I still *really* want a Bloody Mary.

I really don't know what I want.

"Bloody Mary," I blurt out.

She points her finger at me with a sassy finger gun. "You got it. My name is Jade, if you need anything else at all."

"Erin," I say as we shake hands. I'm sitting in 34B, I believe."

"You got it. I'll mix it up and bring it straight to you," she says with a wink.

I meet a cute guy and get a drink before everyone else? Besides the whole getting-locked-in-the-bathroom thing, this is turning into a great flight.

I walk back to my seat, and Landon pops up. He spreads his arms.

"You were saved! The flight attendant had it handled, but I would've stepped in if it would've gone on five more seconds. I enjoy talking to you too much."

I blush as I walk past him. He rubs my shoulder as I pass, and the goosebumps are back.

"I think she was worried the airline would get sued, so I'm even getting a drink early out of it." I pump my fist.

"Nice," Landon says, holding his hand up. I high-five him, and he clasps his fingers over mine. Our eyes lock, and his smile disappears. I do not look away. *Please kiss me, Landon. Make this the most epic flight ever.*

He averts his eyes, and the moment is gone. "You look a lot more comfy."

"Oh yes. I feel like a brand-new woman," I say.

"You got to change, you're getting a drink early, and me? You're having the best flight ever."

I smack him lightly with the back of my hand. "I was just thinking that."

"Erin," Jade, the flight attendant, says. "Here's your Bloody Mary."

"Thank you, Jade," I say, taking the plastic cup brimming with liquid from her. Jade leaves, and I take my first sip. Usually, airplane cocktails leave a lot to be desired. This Bloody Mary is an airplane drink unicorn.

"This is the most amazing Bloody Mary I've ever had. There is so much vodka in this."

"Let me try," Landon asks. I hand him the drink, and he sips, pursing his lips. "Ooh my. I will have to carry you off this plane."

"If I am so lucky," I say, stirring the drink with the plastic toothpick. The drink cart rolls by, and Landon rubs his palms together. I sip my drink. Yes, I want another one, and I want Jade to mix it.

We bounce from topic to topic, ping-ponging and stacking on each other's energy. He tells a lively story about his dog growing up named Spot who made friends with a neighborhood raccoon they named Dot. I laugh so hard I snort unattractively. I tell him about my friends, and I even tell this story about a drunk girl we met in the bathroom in Lake Tahoe and how we steered her toward rekindling things with an ex.

Landon's jaw drops halfway through the story and never closes.

"No way. So, you stayed friends with her?"

"Oh yeah," I say. "Zoey is a riot. We absolutely love her. We got invited to her wedding."

Jade drops off another Bloody Mary for me and an Island Margarita for Landon. He sips it, and his face collapses. My Bloody Mary, while still good, was not as good as the "don't sue us" one was.

"So, Erin," he says, leaning his head against the seat.

"So, Landon," I say. I take another sip. The vodka is doing wonders for my soul.

"I want to know everything about you. First off, are you single?"

"Yes. Incredibly single." I down the last of my drink.

"Oh man. That bad, huh?" Landon asks, and his smile returns.

"I was supposed to get married," I say. "It didn't work out."

"Did you break up before the wedding or..."

"No," I say. Memories from that day come back to me. The night before, Patrick did not respond to my texts after I checked into our bridal suite without him. I remember writing it off since the wine flowed at our rehearsal dinner, and I assumed he had passed out. Patrick was affectionate, kissing my cheek and running his fingertips up and down my bare arm all through the toasts. We walked out to look at the water, and he told me how excited he was to marry me.

Then, I was slipping on my dream dress, about to pull a strap over my shoulder, when Cassie came in with her phone in her hand.

"He's not coming," Cassie said, her eyes filling with tears. I do not remember much after that. Our other friend, Sarah, somehow wrestled me out of my dress, dressed me in sweatpants, and mainlined me vodka. I was a blank slate, devoid of all feelings. It took some time for the tears to come with the intense rage. How could someone be affectionate at a rehearsal dinner and then bail as I pulled on my dress?

"He texted my friend the morning of our wedding and

told her he was not coming," I say. "He did not have the decency to tell me himself. He told my friend."

I say all of this with a finger point; my eyes focused on Landon's lap.

"I'm glad he screwed up, though," Landon says.

I smile, and there is no chance for tears. "What about you?"

"Single," Landon says.

Looking to the ceiling, I smile. "I can't believe this."

"What?" he asks. He waggles his eyebrows, and I want to kiss his lips off, he's so damn cute.

"I get this horrible middle seat, and you waltz onto this plane."

Landon ponders for a moment. "I don't know if I waltzed so much as ran onto this plane like my life depended on it." He pauses. "Maybe I was running to you. Though, I don't believe in that shit."

"What?" I ask.

"Fate. Love at first sight. This is just a happy coincidence."

I'll take it.

He reciprocates my huge grin. I see his slightly crooked teeth that give him a boyish charm. We inch closer to one another, his breath hot on my face. We are so close our foreheads almost touch. My lips almost touch his as I hear, "Oh my God, he's loose!"

3

P lease don't let it be a snake. Please, God, don't let it be a
snake.

Landon and I sit up from our seats, peeking
over the passengers' heads to find other passengers doing
the same thing. Many people scan the aisle, looking for the
loose thing, but I just notice a woman, running down the
aisle, giving zero information, and freaking out.

Jade, the flight attendant, rushes the woman and speaks
in hushed tones as the woman frantically searches under
seats and under other passengers' feet. She begins moving
belongings, and the owners object.

The woman yells out loud, "Zack Morris, where are
you?!"

Landon turns to me. "That is possibly the best name
ever—whatever it is."

I shake my head. "No, it's not. Zack Morris was a total
asshole."

"How dare you shit all over my childhood. Zack Morris
is a legend," Landon says with a wink. His arm is around my
shoulder, his hand grazing my skin. "We will circle back to

your thoughts on the most *delightful character ever*, but first, I need to watch this as it unfolds, second by second. I also need to know what Zack Morris *is*."

Jade and Zack Morris's owner continue to bend down to look under seats. Jade instructs other passengers to stay seated and to alert them if Zack Morris is found.

With all the commotion, there's not a chance in hell anyone will sleep on this flight.

I should really learn my lesson with red-eyes. Tiredness tugs at my eyeballs, and I rub them to alleviate it, but it doesn't help. The adrenaline of the flight and newfound crush on my rowmate mix together in an odd cocktail of alertness.

I may never sleep again.

As the search party wears on, Landon rolls his eyes and stands up, also looking for the elusive animal on the loose. He wanders to the back of the plane, and his face lights up as he crouches down. In hushed baby tones, he coaxes the small creature into his arms. He steps into the aisle and thrusts it above his head.

"I...have...found...ZACK MORRIS."

Above his head, in his hands, is a five-pound, brown Chihuahua.

The owner ambles to him, taking the dog into her arms. She pets the dog as he shivers.

Landon plops back down in the aisle seat. We watch as the owner walks back to her seat, and Jade lowly tells her something we cannot hear. I hope Jade is triple-checking that that dog's carrier is locked.

"That dog was totally looking to escape," Landon says. "Did you see that dog's eyes? They were saying *help me.*"

"I wonder if she dresses him in snazzy shirts in the winter."

"Absolutely," Landon says, grabbing for my hand. "I don't know how I feel about Chihuahuas."

His hand feels nice and soft with mine. I never thought I'd hold hands with a stranger on a plane, multiple times, but here I am.

"Oh, I know how I feel about Chihuahuas. Anything under fifty pounds is not really a dog," I say.

"False," Landon says. "My roommate has a French Bulldog named Mr. Jazzles. Frenchies are the best dogs EVER."

I ponder that for a moment and nod. "Okay, I like those dogs. They are the only small dogs I allow."

"Yes," Landon says with a fist cheer.

I pause for a moment. "This is the craziest flight I've ever been on."

"I usually sleep and avoid everyone, but this flight is different. Special," Landon says, shaking our connected hands on my lap.

"You have been super chatty. You're not like this with everyone?"

Landon shakes his head. "Nope. I mean, I'm *friendly*. Something about traveling, though; I just prefer to keep to myself. This is definitely an anomaly."

"I'm glad I'm your anomaly," I say, patting our hands intertwined between us. "I dare say this is fate, even though you don't believe in it."

"Oh man, now you did it." Landon turns to me, his eyes twinkling with something mischievous. "You mentioned it."

"Don't you think this was fate? Meant to be? We got seated together on this crazy flight? We were destined to meet? It's love at first sight?"

Landon shakes his head. "You're great and all, but no."

I laugh and cover his hand with mine. Landon covers my

hand with his other hand, like we are teammates about to crush a match. Something about Landon being on this flight feels like destiny, like I am meant to be seated next to him.

My day was absolute hell. I cried in the bathroom for ten minutes during a break in negotiations. I wiped the mascara from under my eyes and plastered the bravest face on to finish the meeting; though, inside, I internally screamed. Then, a hunky, Zack Morris-loving, smiley app creator charged the plane, and my day was completely salvaged.

"It feels like you were meant to sit next to me," I say, resting my head on the headrest. "I was having the worst day. You are a ray of light."

He brings his hand to his chest. "Oh, thank you. I do still think this is random."

He leans back as well. "I'm having a great time with you, Erin. Maybe the best time I've ever had on a plane. Truly. I just don't think this is the universe telling me anything. This is just a fun thing that happened."

"You mentioned you were running to me earlier. That has to mean something," I tease.

"Oh, that. It sounded romantic, so I said it. I didn't feel like I was actually running to my destiny. I was legitimately late."

Though I've been disappointed with it, I believe in love. I'm a glutton for punishment.

This thing with Landon is definitely a one-off. A happy accident of a hot, genuine guy seated next to me on an airplane. This could be an experience I reference back to as a moment of magic that only needed to last a few hours to take hold of me forever—even if he claims he doesn't feel the magic.

We did just meet two hours ago.

"Was that an almost kiss earlier?" I ask. I might as well know. It will hurt like hell, but I brace for the answer.

"Oh, I definitely almost kissed you earlier," Landon says. "Just because I don't believe in fate doesn't mean there isn't anything between us. I still want to kiss you."

"Oh good," I say. Our eyes lock again, and I roll my lips together. His lips part slightly, and I want to grab his face and plant a thousand kisses on it. I imagine him undressing me slowly, taking his time as his hands caress my skin, trailing goosebumps along it. My eyelashes flutter with the thought.

This could be the kiss to end all kisses.

That putrid smell from earlier hits me again, and I cringe, closing my eyes. It burns my nostrils, and I gag. I peer around the row of seats, and Smelly Feet Guy is at it again. His feet rest on the armrest. Again.

"Some people, man," Landon says loud enough.

Smelly Feet Guy, who had been quiet the entire plane ride, except the pork-rinds chomping sounds, turns around, glaring at Landon.

"What did you say, Pretty Boy?" Smelly Feet Guy asks.

Oh fucking shit.

"I said, 'Some people, man.' I was talking about you and your feet, bro."

Mild, cautious clapping sounds through the cabin.

"I have a condition. My feet get sweaty on planes since I get overheated."

"Don't we all," Landon says. "My feet feel like they're being waterboarded in the jungle in my shoes right now. I have these stupid wool trainers, and my feet are on FIRE. You don't see me being a dick."

The clapping grows louder.

The balls on Landon. Patrick and other guys I've dated

would've quietly cursed another person like this. Suffer in silence. Seeing Landon stand up for every person on Flight 457 to San Francisco makes my nipples hard.

Smelly Feet Guy unclips his seatbelt and stands up. He is the size of Goliath; his head is close to the top of this airplane. He's wearing a fashion vest.

A full brocade, green-and-pink vest over a black T-shirt.

"Kid, you better watch your mouth."

Landon's eyes go wide. He presses his hand down in the air to the man. "Please be seated."

"Yeah, sit down!" another guy yells from three rows forward. Other passengers turn to watch the commotion and sit up in their seats.

Jade jogs to the man from the rear of the plane. "Hello! Is there anything I can help you with?"

"This little punk is telling me to put my shoes on. I have a condition."

"Your feet stink, man," another guy tells him, waving his hand in front of his nose.

"Sir, I am asking you to sit down," Jade says. I see the back of her head, but the pleading in her voice is real.

He looks flustered, his hands clenching into fists. Landon's hands are up in a universal "don't shoot" pose. Smelly Feet Guy looks around and points a meaty finger at Landon.

"You better be quiet," he says in hushed tones. He walks to his seat, and his butt is *almost* in his seat.

Almost.

Then, Landon opens his big mouth.

"I'll be quiet—when you put your shoes back on."

Everything happens quickly after that. I shift out of the way, practically climbing onto my sleeping neighbor who is jostled awake with the commotion. He blinks like he just resurfaced from a coma.

Here's what I think happened: Smelly Feet Guy stood up, wound up, and clobbered Landon in the face. Something goes flying from Landon, and it lands on my thigh, perfectly in the lip of my shirt.

I grab it before it goes flying, and it's a *fucking* tooth.

There's a flurry of limbs and bodies. A man wedges himself between Landon and Smelly Feet Guy, and Smelly Feet Guy screeches.

"You stepped on my foot!" he yells when Landon just lost a tooth.

"Oh shit, oh shit, oh shit!" I say. I clasp it in my hand as two men—one of them being Landon—wrestles Smelly Feet Guy to the ground. Another man steps in, and they haul the brute of a man to the rear of the plane. They rearrange groggy passengers from the back row, moving one person to Smelly Feet Guy's original spot. A tank of a man steps in and sits on the aisle while Smelly Feet Guy is shoved next to the window.

Jade, the flight attendant, scurries around, running from the front of the plane to the back of the plane. She talks to Landon, examining his face each direction. She runs off and returns with a plastic bag of ice.

Landon turns around with a bruised lip and a big smile. A tooth from his bottom row is missing. He smacks the bag of ice to his lip and gives me a thumbs up.

My mouth stretches in horror. I don't understand how Landon has so much chill right now.

"What?" he asks.

I hold up the tooth in the palm of my hand. A light whine echoes from my mouth.

"Oh," he says, plucking it from my hand. "Thanks! Those things are expensive."

My forehead scrunches in confusion. "What?"

"It's a fake tooth," Landon says. "I lost my original one when I played hockey. Cliché, I know." He clasps it between two fingers.

My breath shallows, and Landon cups my anxiety-hitched shoulder. "It's really not that big of a deal. It's not the first time it's been knocked loose. To be honest, this is not my first fight."

"I have so many questions," I say.

"Ladies and gentlemen, this is your captain speaking," a man's voice announces over the intercom. "Unfortunately, since we had an incident, we will have to divert to the nearest airport. We ask you to remain calm and seated with your seatbelt fastened. We will hopefully get you back on your way to San Francisco with minimal delays."

Lots of yelling and chattering erupt over the plane. Jade stops every few rows to answer questions. There's lots of complaining, and I notice one lucky son-of-a-bitch is still passed out with his mouth wide open.

Everyone is upset. All because Landon stood up to a man with hot, sweating feet.

I've never witnessed anything sexier.

"When were you in fights before?" I ask, resting my arm on his shoulder.

Landon shrugs and says, "I once saw this guy who would not leave this woman alone at a bar. I approached him, and the woman told me he was an ex-boyfriend who couldn't accept they were broken up. The man punched me, so I punched him back. Sprained my hand, but it was totally worth it."

It doesn't make sense what I do next. I do it anyway.

I grab his face and kiss him.

"Ow," he yelps as my lips touch his. I pull away, and he breaks into a smile. "Just kidding. I'm a tank."

He grabs my face and kisses me softly, and the world falls away.

4

Y kiss with Landon is the absolute peak of this flight. After the kiss, all hell breaks loose, and it's rolling downhill into a pile of shit.

Someone delirious from sleep deprivation rants about the plane landing, mentioning a granddaughter they haven't seen in two years. Others complain how this ruins plans, how their whole day is ruined.

We were going to land in the middle of the night, but okay.

Jade still works for every penny of her meager salary by calming irate passenger after irate passenger. Smelly Feet Guy is still barricaded successfully by a large man who obviously lifts. Landon and I begin taking bets on who might cry when landing or if Grandma will stand up with clenched fists since she feels moved by the spirit of her rant.

"People are the absolute worst," Landon says. "Smelly Feet Guy...that lady." He points to the front of the plane. Grandma still loudly proclaims her dissatisfaction with this flight.

"We can just make out until this plane lands," I suggest.

He runs his palm against the back of my neck. I know now what the connection truly feels like, how it warms me to my toes and through my limbs. My entire body is on high alert.

"Oh really," Landon says. "With this crowd, don't you think they will complain?"

"Oh, absolutely." I point to my other rowmate, who is awake, wearing large headphones and watching a dark window. If he could crawl into the wall, he would in a second. "I feel bad for him."

"I feel bad for all of us."

"You were the one who instigated a fight. This is, technically, your fault," I tease, poking Landon in the stomach.

"Hey, he was gassing people with his feet. What was I supposed to do?"

Then, a woman turns around in front of us. We have not heard a peep from her this entire flight, but now we see her arched, painted-on eyebrows and puffy hair.

"Thank you so much for telling that guy off. I have asthma, and the stench was slowly killing me."

"See?!" Landon screeches, holding his hands out. "You're welcome, ma'am."

His politeness ignites another part of me.

"Just kiss me already," I say.

"Well, okay." His lips touch mine again, and all the chatter and activity falls away.

We fall into a trance, like a couple of high school kids at a house party. The captain interrupts our dream momentarily.

"Ladies and gentlemen, we are waiting for clearance to divert to Waterloo Regional Airport. The local authorities have been contacted and will board the plane once we have landed. Please remain seated until I instruct that you are allowed to move about the cabin."

"You're a goner," I say. "You're definitely going off this plane in handcuffs."

The woman in front of us turns back again. She says, "I will vouch for you. The other guy struck first."

"See? At least you have faith in me," he says to the woman.

"Of course! How long have you two been together?" The woman waggles her pointer finger between us.

"Oh, we just met," I say.

"I don't even know her middle name," Landon says. He watches my eyes, waiting for me to offer it.

I just want to be coy. Enough of me has been vulnerable on this flight.

"Nope," I say. "You have to earn the middle name. It's embarrassing."

"Well, I will tell you mine. It's Bernard."

"Landon Bernard Walcott," I say. "Definitely has a ring to it."

"Erin Blank Campbell. Has a ring to it," he says.

"You seem perfect for each other!" the woman says. "It must be fate. I always love a good love story. Have you seen the movie *Serendipity*? One of my favorites!"

When we don't answer her, she turns around slowly.

"She had to bring up fate." He shakes his head.

"Are you serious right now? How is this not fate? Not meant to happen?"

Landon rests his head against the headrest. "I have met some wonderful people. Randomly. I do not really believe people come into your life for a reason or it was meant to happen. We are all trying to figure it out on our own, look for meaning in randomness, and there isn't. All you have to do is live your life with integrity and seize opportunities as they present themselves. I am the master of my own destiny that I create. It wasn't created for me. There's no grand plan for me, or you, or anyone else in the universe."

"So, what happens when we finally get to San Francisco?" I brace for the answer.

"We'll see what happens," he says, kissing the tip of my nose. He intertwines his fingers with mine over the armrest as we watch the chaos unfold as the plane feels suspended in the air, making tiny movements forward.

Continuing to canoodle with Landon is a bad idea. I know myself, and this situation just spells disaster. A hopeless romantic, I have already pictured the future with this stranger who became a kissing partner. I have tried (and failed) many times to lower my expectations for people, meet men where they are, but I inevitably go to rainbows and happily ever afters.

Maybe this meeting on a plane is completely random and should be treated as such. So, when my sister has babies and they ask, "Auntie, what is the craziest thing to happen to you?" I can reference this flight. I can talk about a dashing app designer who stood up to a man with horrific-smelling feet, how Zack Morris the Chihuahua ran away from his owner, and how we ended up in Iowa. How I never saw Landon again after this, but it was perfect as a brief love affair.

Once he leaves the plane, he will wave, and San Francisco will swallow him, never to reappear in my life. He will be something I constantly question about reality. Did this magic really happen? Did I get seated next to the most engaging, wittiest, funniest man just for him to slip away?

My heart aches, but I know that I must prepare myself

now. He thinks this is random. He thinks this is not meant to be.

I must think the same—no matter how much everything in my body says this is right.

The captain eventually gets clearance after it feels like we've been circling for an hour. When we finally land, it is the smoothest landing I've ever experienced. Instead of cheering, the landing elicits loud groans and sounds of dissatisfaction.

The authorities immediately appear and remove Smelly Feet Guy. I thought it would be exciting, but really, he goes peacefully. They lead him off in handcuffs, and there are baby cheers in the crowd. Shoeless and ashamed, he disappears from the plane. The angst in the passengers dissipates. For now.

We sit in a murmur of chatter as passengers wait for the plane to take off again.

"How long until we take off again, do you think?" I ask.

"At least two hours. Saddle up," Landon says. "We should ask each other questions."

"Right," I say. Scanning my mind, all I can come up with is, "What's your favorite food?"

"Sushi," Landon says. "What about you?"

"Pizza," I say. "Very basic."

"Pizza is a classic," he says. "Least favorite food?"

"Um, kale. It's not good. You?"

"Chocolate mousse."

I sit back, aghast. I did not see that coming. "Why?"

"The texture," he says, shaking his head with his tongue outstretched. "Also, I had a traumatic experience with a frenemy in elementary school who smeared it all over my butt at a birthday party. Everyone thought I shit my pants. For the record, I *did not* shit my pants."

"Fair enough," I say.

"Favorite thing to do in the city?"

"I love coffee shops attached to bookstores. If I have a weekend afternoon free, I get a latte and peruse the shelves. I could be there for hours."

"Nice," Landon says. "Place you've always wanted to visit?"

I know immediately. "The Santorini Islands in Greece."

Landon nods. I also add, "Barcelona. Italy. Basically all over Europe."

"Europe is so fun and beautiful. Have you ever been there?"

I shake my head. "It's just a dream at this point, I guess. I barely have enough money to afford an apartment in the city. I have no idea when I'll have money to travel."

We sit quietly, and Landon leans out into the aisle.

"What do you think is taking so long?" He checks his watch. "It's been forty-five minutes."

I check my watch as well. We should've been home by now.

Cassie. Oh dear God, I need to let her know.

I awaken my phone and find my text thread with Cassie. I explain the situation, that we were grounded, and I have no idea when we will get home. Then, I drop a juicy nugget.

Erin: I am also seated next to the dreamiest, nicest, cutest guy ever. WE MADE OUT.

I turn my phone over. A smirk crosses my lips.

"You are up to something," he says.

"I just told my roommate about you," I say.

"You did. What did you say?"

"Wouldn't you like to know?" My phone vibrates, and I turn it over.

Cassie: pictures or it didn't happen

"She wants a picture of you," I tell him.

"Well, let's give this roommate what she wants." Landon purses his lips and squints one eye with an arched brow. Laughing, I snap the photo and send it to my friend.

Cassie: dear lord he is cute

Me: I know right???!!! I have no idea when I'll be home. Go to bed. I'll make it home okay.

Cassie: Are you sure?

Me: Positive

I slip my phone back into my carry-on and turn to Landon, whose chin is propped on his hands.

"Everything okay?"

"Yeah," I say. "I'll have to find my own way home—whenever we get home."

"I can take you," he offers. "I left my car at SFO."

"That's really sweet of you, but you don't have to…"

He silences me with his pointer finger against my lips. "We have already swapped spit and bonded over several things. Zack Morris. Smelly Feet. You survived a stuck bathroom door situation. The least I can do is drive you home."

"Okay," I say. I pause before I say the next bit. "You'll know where I live. We can't test fate."

"I don't want to test fate; I want to see you again. So, I want to know where you live. I would like your phone number—if you want to give me that information, of course."

"I do want you to have it," I say.

"Good," he says. "May I kiss you again? It's been at least an hour."

I nod, and he kisses me again, holding my chin. Our lips move together, in perfect sync, and it's just him and me in this dance of tongues and lips.

The woman in the row in front of us sighs. She cannot

see us since her face is forward. I wonder if she is holding up a phone in selfie mode so she can see.

More time passes, more kisses, and more speculation.

This whole time, we had a celebrity on the flight.

Savannah Watson, up-and-coming country star, stands up with her guitar and comes into coach to play to the masses. She plays her beautiful hit single "Home Again," and everyone cheers. She even plays some Dolly Parton. I've never been a country fan, but anything at this point is entertaining.

A crowd huddles ten rows up, near where Zack Morris's owner sits. I wonder if people are so bored they're petting a petrified Chihuahua.

More time passes. I feel like I will die on this plane. Jade empties her entire snack supply to anyone who asks. I have had so many stale plane pretzels I'm as swollen as a balloon.

Then, the announcement everyone has been waiting for.

"Ladies and gentlemen, this is your captain speaking. The plane is having mechanical issues, so we will be deboarding the plane and placing you in accommodations for the night. We deeply apologize for the inconvenience."

"Oh my God," I say. "I've never been to Iowa."

"I have been once. Nice people. I have never heard of Waterloo."

"This is the wildest flight I've ever been on."

"At least there's some closure," Landon says. "We can finally get off this plane."

"True," I say.

It takes almost as long to get off the plane as it took sitting there on the tarmac. I grab my day bag full of my suit, and Landon grabs his carry-on. When we reach the front of the plane, he reaches back and grabs my hand.

A motel room. A bed. I sure hope this means what I

5

Somehow, we end up at a small motel on the outskirts of town since Waterloo didn't expect a planeful of people to touch down and need rooms for the night. It is so dark and we're surrounded by cornfields that creepy children can walk out of, at any moment.

I do not know how this is being paid for or how we ended up here. My eyelids grow heavy with each change, my body shutting down as a mutiny against what my brain wants.

And what my vagina wants.

I recognize a few others from the plane in this tiny lobby. An older gentleman holding a John Grisham hardback with his arms wrapped tightly around him. A young couple huddled together since this room is *freezing*. The doors keep opening, bringing with it a gust of wind that chills me.

It's the only thing keeping me awake.

We let the man go, and then we let the couple go. Landon winks at me, like everything is going to be okay. His hand has not left my hand since we left the plane. Together.

When it is finally our turn, the motel clerk holds up his

hand. "Are you together? I only have one room left. With one bed."

"I...uh," I say, and then Landon steps forward.

"I can just go back to the airport. It's fine," he says. I hear him whisper under his breath, "I just hope Uber operates this late in this town."

"Landon, come to my room." My heart beats wildly in my chest as he looks up with a complex swirl of emotions on his face. He doesn't know if it's a good idea. He might think it's a great idea.

"I'm not imposing..."

"Absolutely not," I say, and I turn back to the motel clerk. "We're together."

"Okay," he says, punching in numbers. They ask for a credit card, and Landon steps in since the airline promised accommodations. It is all sorted in front of me, and I cannot register the outcome.

All I know is it's nice to be taken care of.

When we get the keys, Landon takes my luggage like the gentleman he is. We find our room at the absolute opposite end of the white building. Some rooms are quiet; some still have the TV blaring. We pass a room where faint moans waft out of the windows, and I blush.

Would that be us?

"This is it," he says, pushing the keycard into the slot. It takes a couple tries before the door beeps and we are inside our room for the night.

One king-sized bed in the middle of the room.

"I'll take the floor," Landon blurts out immediately.

"It's fine. The bed looks big enough." I sit down, my body responding to the moment of rest. If I sit for too long, I will curl up and fall asleep, ruining any chances of sex with

this enigmatic stranger. Looking at the carpet, I will definitely put socks on.

Landon crosses his arms, scanning the room.

"This is less than ideal," he says.

My cheeks flush. Does he mean the quality of the
room, or...

"It's fine, I..."

"I'm hungry," he blurts out, pulling at his wallet in his
jeans. "It's been a while since I had questionable vending
machine food. Do you want anything? A soda? More
pretzels?"

I laugh.

"Whatever you get is fine," I say. Landon walks toward
me and kisses me awkwardly on the head. He leaves, and I
am left alone.

My mother would be flapping her arms in anxiety.

Her daughter, left at the altar, forced to share a room
with an accomplished app designer who does not believe in
fate and probably does not believe in romance.

I stand up to wake myself up, jumping tiny jumps to
wake up my limbs. No, we are not falling asleep just because
we are in a room with a bed. I am going to bang this beautiful man who we may never see again, because I need this.

Oh, how I need this.

I walk to the sinks and splash some cool water on my
face. Anything to wake myself up. Did Landon act weird
before he left?

Noooo. That can't be it.

The worry wakes me up like a shot of caffeine straight to
my veins.

Maybe he isn't into this now that we're off the plane.
Maybe he's freaking out. We are sharing the same room

now, but that wasn't his choice. He wanted to go back to the airport, but he is staying here. With me.

He doesn't believe in instant connections or fate. He might think we're moving too fast. He may get skittish and bolt. Did he just bolt? He's been gone for a long time.

I have no idea where he would go so late in a town he doesn't know, but I had a man run away from me who I knew pretty well. Anything is possible.

I pace, working on my path in the carpet, checking my watch. If I had his number, I would've texted him three times already. I let out a sigh of relief when he arrives back with snacks exploding from his arms.

"I had a bunch of singles and change so I got a little bit of everything. I have no idea how old this food is. I wasn't sure what you liked. Oh, and..." He hands me a Diet Coke.

"Thank you," I say, popping off the top. The fake-sugar taste hits my teeth, and I feel rejuvenated.

He spreads the snacks across the turquoise-and-orange bedspread. All the favorites are here. I take a bag of Fritos and crack it open. The chips are fresh and crisp between my teeth. He grabs a Snickers bar.

"It's been a while, my love," he says to the Snickers, unwrapping it and taking a delicious bite. His eyes close in ecstasy. "Not stale. A win."

Not completely sure if I will be seeing that face later.

"This feels like a movie," I say as I crumple the bag in my hand and throw it in the trash.

"Absolutely," he says. He smiles and winks, and everything is okay again.

"Has this ever happened to you?" I ask, sitting down on the bed. The soda and the chips have given me life, and I feel semi-awake. For now.

"No," he says with a laugh, taking the last bite.

He sits down, facing me, our knees touching. "This is not fate, though."

"Of course not," I say with a wink to match his.

"I just happen to be seated next to the most beautiful woman I have ever seen," he says, placing his hand on my knee, like a test. I look up at him, and his eyes plead with me.

With hesitation, I lean in, touching his cheek with just my fingertips. Our lips touch softly, sensually, and he responds. His lips take mine, and we are back to our effortless connection—strong, easy. My body moves forward toward him like a magnet to another, and his hands press into my upper back. Somehow, I'm straddling him with my arms wrapped around his neck.

It has been so long since I had romance, so long since I felt a man's touch on my skin. It feels better than I remember, full of hopeful electricity.

The kisses take my breath, and I pull away to gulp air. I can feel his hard length through my thin leggings, and the friction between us is enough to drive me insane. He takes a strand of hair and tucks it behind my ear. His eyes connect to mine.

"Where did you come from?" he asks, his eyes burrowing into mine.

"San Francisco," I say like a complete dork.

Landon laughs with his whole body and steals a kiss. "You are so goddamn cute."

We kiss again, and he rolls me onto my back with his lanky frame between my legs. He dives down on me, kissing my lips, my neck, my collarbone. All the sensations fire, and my mind short-circuits with all the new feelings reawakened inside of me.

This is what I miss the most from being in love.

Landon pulls back from me and hovers over me. Something brews behind those eyes, something I do not know. All I know is that this feels right.

"I don't have anything," he finally admits.

Well, fuck.

"Oh," is all I say as I sit up.

"I know," he says, rubbing his hair. "I have no idea what is even open in Waterloo at this hour."

I remember the small area next to the motel clerk, an area full of meager snacks and toiletries. "Did you go to the general-store area next to the motel clerk?"

Landon's face scrunches in confusion. "No. I found a vending machine in the middle of the building."

"I wonder if they have condoms," I say.

"They could," he says, and then he slaps his hands. "Adventure time!"

He high-fives me, and while it is unsexy, it's so endearing it becomes downright erotic.

"I'm ready," I say. I grab a cardigan from my carry-on to throw over my T-shirt and leggings. I pull my flats on over my socks, which is awkward, but we're going to the lobby.

The motel clerk has probably seen a lot worse.

The night is ink black with only the odd light from a far-off farm to illuminate the cracked parking lot. We walk quietly, while other patrons do not have the same courtesy. We hear moaning from a different room, and then, we hear screaming from another.

The bell shutters with noise when we enter the lobby, and the motel clerk is nowhere to be found.

"Over here," Landon says with a finger point. Together, we walk to the picked-over grocery section. There are pretzels (I'm not sure I can ever eat another pretzel at this point), and a shit-ton of pain relievers.

No condoms.

"Damn," Landon says, looking in all the nooks and crannies.

"It wasn't meant to be, I guess," I say.

"You stop that right now. That's quitter talk," he says.

"What, the fate talk?" I ask with innocence, but he looks at me and rolls his eyes.

Just then, the motel clerk emerges from the back.

"See, a sign," I say.

Landon glares at me again but leans in. "Let's see if my charm wins."

"Go for it," I say.

He clears his voice for the motel clerk and leans on the counter. "Excuse me, good sir."

"Yes?" the motel clerk asks, looking up.

"Do you, by chance, have any condoms for purchase?"

The motel clerk looks in the general area of the grocery but then shrugs his shoulders. "The other couple with you cleaned me out of my personal stash about five minutes ago. I wouldn't trust them, though." We wait for more elaboration, but nothing.

"Where is the nearest gas station?" I ask.

The motel clerk looks to the ceiling for answers. "It's close, about five miles."

Landon leans toward me and whispers, "That is not close."

"Maybe that's Iowa-close," I say.

"Good point." Landon smacks the counter with an open palm. "We will be on our way then."

"You do that," he says.

The night air blasts us in the face upon our exit.

"Damn," Landon says.

Breathing in and out, I summon whatever courage I have

to suggest something that makes my palms sweat. "You know, there are other things we can do."

Landon quirks an eyebrow. "Like what?"

"If you are free of disease, I wouldn't mind..." I pop out my cheek with my tongue.

"Oh...OH," Landon says, pondering it with his chin in his hand. "Well, we must make it fair. You first."

"Excellent," I say as we scamper back to our room. When we get back, his hands are at the base of my neck, his breath hot on my ear. Our kisses become frantic, full of heat and urgency, and my shirt is off with just my boring basic bra that gapes from my chest.

He palms them, and my body responds. I sit back on the bed, and he crawls toward me, gripping my leggings and peeling them away slowly.

I'm so glad I shaved my legs last night.

He says nothing as he kisses my belly and unhooks my bra, looking at my breasts like he has uncovered a pile of gold. His tongue rolls over my nipple as I buck under his hand that cradles my sensitive area.

I rub his hair as I lie there. The sensations are everything, and I don't know which to focus on first.

His kisses lighten as he snakes down my body, his lips inches from my sex, ready and wet for him. One finger enters me and then two. Then, his mouth is on me, and it shoots pleasure through me, radiating to all my corners. Moaning has always been a performative act for me, but these are genuine, coming from deep recesses within my core.

This man...where did he come from?

His tongue laps at my clit perfectly, and I build quickly to an orgasm that rips through me, sending shutters of pleasure so intense I almost roll off the bed.

Landon stands, wiping his mouth, and I feel another wave of desire.

After the aftershocks have rolled out of me, I sit up, pulling him toward me by his belt loops.

"My turn," I say, unbuckling his belt.

"You don't have to," he says.

Oh, now I'm definitely doing it.

He doesn't protest much longer as I unzip his pants. He is already long and thick. Inside, I'm also crying. Why couldn't there be one questionable condom in the whole motel?

The orgasm was amazing, but it would've been more amazing to have Landon inside me.

Starting with the head, I flick my tongue against it slowly, and Landon responds. He leans toward me, and I take him deeper into my mouth. Bobbing my head, his breath quickens, and he moves with me, matching my rhythm. I bring my hand to his balls, and he responds. Looking up at him, I see this beautiful man I just met and I love knowing that I have this effect on him.

His hands lightly rest on my head, and he says breathlessly, "I'm going to come."

I do not pull away but, instead, lock his eyes with mine. That connection unravels him.

Salty liquid hits the back of my throat. I swallow dutifully and pull away.

His eyes are closed as he stands there, teetering on his heels. He kisses me, although each other is still on our lips, and it's a kiss of shared experience, of connection.

"That took the stuffing right out of me."

I giggle at his turn of phrase, and he smiles. He asks while smiling, "What?"

"Stuffing. It's cute," I say with a snicker.

"Yeah, glad I said that *after.*"

"No, it's endearing," I say.

"Let's not think about how unclean these sheets are and get to bed."

"Sounds great."

The sheets are softer than they appear when we climb in. Landon pulls me toward him so I'm the little spoon. He grips me and buries his head in the crook of my neck.

"Sorry, I'm a snuggler," he says.

"Completely fine with me," I reply.

So funny to go from crying in the bathroom during a break from a job I hate to having oral sex with a man I barely know in a random motel room in Iowa.

A complete stranger that has become more familiar to me than men I'd been with for years.

Landon might not believe it, but this feels like more than just a random coincidence that we were seated next to each other.

No matter what he says, this feels like fate. It feels like love at first sight. It's everything we tell little girls not to expect.

6

The buzzing of my phone wakes me from my coma. It was the kind of sleep where I completely forgot where I was. It startles me, actually, but the memories of the night before come flooding back, and the panic leaves me.

Landon is still here, asleep, with one arm across my middle.

My phone vibrates, and I check the screen. It's my boss, Daryl.

"Hello," I say once my fingers stop fumbling and I can press talk.

"Erin, thank God. I've been trying to call you. Where are you? I heard what happened."

"I'm in Iowa. In a motel."

"Oh, poor thing; I'm so sorry."

I don't mention that I'm not the least bit sorry. I push my hair from my face. "What's up?"

"The Coffer Group, they called me. They're not sure about the deal. Supposedly, they got another offer, and it looks good to them, too, and they're floundering. I need you to go back to New York. They like you, and I think you can close it. It is just really unfortunate you are in Iowa."

"Can I call them? Maybe that can work. I have no idea when I can get a flight to New York. I mean, it's Iowa."

"The other offer came local, so someone in New York. Listen, I really need you to get back there. Stay as long as you need to. *Close this deal.* If you close this deal, the promotion we've been discussing might happen sooner than later."

I pause for a second. I've been asking for a raise and promotion consistently for years. When I think about how much money I've made the company and how little has trickled down, I could scream.

It doesn't matter that I cry in bathrooms during work. It doesn't matter that I just met the most interesting, soul-connecting man I have ever met. This is business, and this is my life.

Landon is just a guy I had fun with once, who did not believe in fate, though my body screams that *yes, this is fate.*

"Okay, I'll go." I have no idea how I will get back to New York or even to the airport.

Landon stirs next to me when I kiss his cheek. One eye cracks open, and he looks at me.

"Morning, sunshine," I say. "I have to go."

That wakes him up. He sits straight up and rubs his eyes. "What?"

"My boss called me. The deal is about to fall through, and I need to go back to New York."

The expression on Landon's face can be described as blank. "Okay," he says.

I breathe in and out. I do not want to be the typical woman who jumps all over a man for a response of one word. Still, it hurts me that there is not more angst, more desire from him.

We sit there at a standstill. I break, standing up and walking over to my luggage.

He says nothing as I pull out my rumpled suit and examine what I'm dealing with. Landon says nothing as I search and eventually find the iron. As it warms on the ironing board I found, I check for flights out of Waterloo to New York.

When I turn back, Landon sits cross-legged on the bed, cracking his knuckles. It feels like we're strangers again—something I keep forgetting.

His stare bores into me, even with my back to him. I turn around and shrug. "What?"

"I wanted more time with you," he says.

"Well, I have to work. The deal may fall through, and they want me back in New York. I have to go."

"But it seems like you hate your job."

"I don't *hate* it," I say as I hold my hand a little from the iron. It's finally hot enough.

It helps distract from the awkwardness and the general anxiety.

"When I first sat down next to you, you seemed so uncomfortable. It's just something I noticed."

He is not wrong. It makes me want to crawl out of my skin. My parents always raised me to believe that work is not supposed to be fun. It's called work for a reason, so you find something you're good at, excel at it, and that will fulfill you.

A stranger sees something in me that my friends don't see and my parents do not comment on. My brain spins with his words.

"I'm good at it. And I'm vital to my company."

"You just seemed like a very unhappy person when I sat down. That is, until we started talking, and then you came to life. It was nice to see."

That comment strips me bare.

This man, who does not believe in fate or destiny, has an unknown level of heartbreak in store for me. Patrick, so steadfast, blindsided me on our wedding day when everything about our relationship felt safe and comforting. Landon is uncertainty incarnate, and I cannot take it, known or unknown.

"Maybe I just want you to fly back to San Francisco with me. Spend more time together."

"And then what?" I ask as I run the iron over my blazer pockets. Working on the creases is the perfect distraction.

"And then...I don't know." His honesty hits me in the gut. He is basically asking me to quit my job just so we can spend a few more hours together. There are no declarations of love or passion from this man I've known less than twenty-four hours.

That kind of thing only happens in movies, but I still hope and pine for it like a silly, silly woman.

I prop up the iron and turn around. "I have to go for my job. I can't just get on a plane with you, and go back hand-in-hand, and then we never see each other again. Are we together now..."

"No," he says bluntly. He stands up and approaches me, and I recoil away from his outstretched hands. His brow furrows. "But I would like to see where this goes."

"Ah," I say, putting my hands on my hips. I laugh, at the ground.

What should I expect out of this man I just met? I have no idea.

"Erin," he says softly, reaching for me again.

So many things came to me after Patrick left. All the signs I did not see. The red flags that slapped me in the face, and I did not register them.

Here, a man tells me that he doesn't believe in fate, we are not together. I would be a complete idiot to not see this for what it is.

Not fate. Not even a blip on the great loves of my life. This was just a tryst in a rundown motel in Iowa. Something to pass the time, something fun to tell my friends when I go back to San Francisco.

"Let's just call this what it was. A distraction," I say.

"Erin, I..." Landon says, and then my phone buzzes again.

Daryl.

"I have to take this," I say as I point to my phone.

Daryl is breathless. "Hi, so Charlotte was able to find a flight out of Waterloo that lays over in Chicago, but you could be in New York by one. I need you at the airport immediately."

"Got it," I say. "Email me the flight info."

"She already did it," Daryl says.

"Thanks, boss," I say. I end the call and chuck my phone across the room. I finish ironing the pants to the best they're going to be and take all the clothes into the bathroom.

Now that this is on the verge of ending, Landon seeing me naked is too much since we are about to become strangers.

When I walk out, Landon stands in the same spot. His indifferent stance tells me everything I need to know.

"I'll come to the airport with you. I should see what's going on with the flight to San Francisco anyway."

"Okay," I say.

"We can just chalk this up to a fun flight and a fun night," Landon says. I expect him to smile at his rhyme, but it does not register.

"I think so," I say.

He crosses his arms, and his eyes look everywhere but at me. "I mean, this wasn't meant to be forever. This wasn't fate."

"No," I agree.

"Okay," he agrees.

How quickly he gives up on this is my answer. This was nothing to him.

There's something in his eyes that is confusing, and I can't quite put my finger on it.

We collect our belongings quickly, and Landon checks us out as I call a cab. The morning air is crisp on my skin; fall has arrived. The seasons barely change in San Francisco, so it's nice to see the season, even for a moment.

I choose to focus on this moment. Not that it is ending, but that it happened.

This will be a good memory to take me through the rest of my life.

Something gnaws at me, though, when Landon walks toward me with a nod. His eyes look heavy and red, and he sniffles as he takes me in his arms and says nothing. I wrap my arms around him in response, and we settle in together. He kisses my hair just as the cab arrives.

Landon takes my luggage from me and puts it in the trunk.

The pangs begin in my chest as I sit there next to Landon. He grips my hand even though we are not meant to be, and it makes my heart soar and ache all at the same time.

Landon rushed into my life unexpectedly, and now he is leaving it forever.

It's silly to say, but he changed me.

When we reach the airport, I pull up the reservation details that Charlotte emailed me. I check in and get my boarding pass as Landon checks in with Skyline on alternatives to get him to San Francisco.

I wait for him, although my flight is boarding soon.

I have to.

He finally finishes and approaches me.

"This was so great," he says, taking my arms in his hands. "I am so glad we were seated together."

"Me too," I say. I do not ask when we will see each other again. I wait for him to ask for my number, but he doesn't. With a smile, I say, "I guess we'll just leave it up to fate, huh?"

"I guess," he says. "You can finally prove to me that fate is real."

He kisses me tenderly, softly, with a caress of my cheek.

The announcements shake me from this dream. I need to go.

I walk away, and my heart cannot take it. This feels wrong. Why didn't he ask for my phone number? It feels like I'm floating as I make my way through security and to my gate. I make it just in time.

When I'm seated, I have women on either side of me. I'm back in my uncomfortable suit, heading to do a job I hate, and away from a man I could've seen a future with after less than twenty-four hours.

I cannot help it. I begin to sob.

7

Usually, Mondays are always a bitch, but this Monday...

This Monday is a big ol' bitch.

I take the bus to my stop, three blocks from my office. I am cornered by two homeless people who will not give up, and everything smells worse than Smelly Feet Guy's feet.

The breeze kicks up, freezing me in my bones, and I pull open my office building's door. The lobby is unnecessarily warm, probably a knee-jerk reaction to the cold outside, and I sweat instantly in my blazer.

I had closed the deal after hours of grueling negotiation. Daryl called in, and we closed it together. The papers had been signed, and I got a virtual pat on the back.

Usually, I would feel great victory and satisfaction at a job well done.

However, I became the cliché I hated: a woman pining after a man who didn't want her.

Landon was so perfect on the plane, completely into me and reactive. His kisses told me he wanted me, and our time in the motel felt magical. He had carved a hollow hole within me, and I felt barren when he didn't ask to see me, didn't arrange a time, didn't put my number in his phone.

He had been clear, though. This was not fate. This was not meant to be. We did not experience love at first sight.

It shattered me. I still feel broken as I climb the stairs to the third floor. I don't trust elevators.

I open the door to our suite to see a new receptionist. The spot never stays filled for long. Today it is a white woman with puffy gray hair and chains linked to her glasses. I smile and introduce myself.

My cubicle is in a dead pocket of the office, facing a corner of a wall. Only the offices have views of other gray buildings. I drop all my stuff, my backpack, my lunch, my coffee mug.

This cubicle feels small.

Grabbing my heels, I sit down and slip out of my sneakers and slip the uncomfortable leather onto my feet.

"Knock, knock," Daryl says, propping his forearms on my cubicle's top.

"Hey, Daryl," I say, the weariness audible in my voice.

"You don't look so good."

"Well, last week was long."

"You didn't work this weekend, though. I was hoping you could've emailed *a little bit* more," he says, holding his forefinger and thumb an inch apart.

I slept all weekend because my body shut down completely. Daryl told me not to worry about working so I stare at him.

"We have a team meeting at nine in my office," Daryl says. He snaps his fingers at me, and I scream on the inside. "See you there!"

"Of course," I say. I fire up my computer and make a quick to-do list for the day. The words on the computer swim as I blink to focus my eyes. Rubbing my temples does absolutely nothing. The coffee does nothing.

Being back in this office will get better. I will get back into the routine, and everything will be fine.

We closed the deal.

This promotion is mine.

Then, I will get a nice office with sunlight, where I'll pile well-loved books on a shelf, and swivel in a chair whenever someone comes to my door.

I think about this until nine for our meeting.

"I want everyone to congratulate Erin on closing the Coffer Group," Daryl says with an initiating applause. The rest of my coworkers give unenthusiastic claps as I press my lips into a hard line. "She was stranded in Iowa due to a plane delay and then got back on a plane, laid over, and got back to our new acquisition to close the deal. Everyone take note...this is what dedication looks like."

My coworkers sneer at me, and I don't blame them.

This office is competitive to a fault; no one cheers another's successes.

I can't wait to be out of the trenches and in an office, just like this one.

"Erin, can you hang back?" Daryl asks after the meeting ends. I nod, and my stomach churns.

Here we go. Moment of truth.

He motions for me to sit, and I smooth out my skirt before perching on the chair's end. He closes the door and then sits on the edge of the desk, feet away from me.

"I cannot tell you enough how excellent you did in New York."

"Thank you, sir. It was my pleasure."

"So," he says. He stands up and walks to his office chair.

He licks his thumb to open a folder. "I have a new project for you."

He pushes a paper to me.

"Sir, I was curious about the promotion. You mentioned that over the phone..."

"Oh," he says, pushing away my idea like it's a fly. "Not right now. There isn't a spot available for you to take."

My stomach churns harder. My palms sweat at the thought of what I have to do.

Confrontation.

This has been coming for years, like a slow-moving train. I could've gotten out of the way of it at any time, but I didn't. I willingly stayed here, watching the bright light come closer and closer.

"Besides, you are a better foot soldier. You don't want to do what I do. You like to get your hands dirty. Shake the hands, revel in the thrill of negotiation."

"But.." I say, stumbling over my words. The stomach churning morphs into full-blown cramps.

"So this new project, much easier than the one you just closed..."

My throat goes dry, and the room spins.

Landon knew what I didn't know.

I fucking hate this job.

I always thought work is work. It's something everyone hates. But not everyone hates what they do.

Landon doesn't. My roommate left a job she hated and now she's doing what she loves.

Even Zoey, the random girl I met in a club bathroom in South Lake Tahoe, found a job she loves.

It becomes clear to me. Crystal, even.

I stand up, and Daryl barely glances up. I wait for his

eyes to meet mine, and I cross my arms since it feels uncomfortable to wait.

"What?" he asks. "You can review it at your desk, if you would like."

Closing my eyes, I center myself. Breathe in, breathe out. The silence hangs uncomfortably.

"I don't think I can work here anymore," I blurt out.

His glance is full-perturbed. I uncross my arms and balance my fingertips on the desk.

"Well, I'm sorry you feel that way," Daryl says. "You're one of our best."

I don't know what I was expecting. Maybe some grand gesture. Maybe some, "Just kidding. We were totally going to give you that promotion!"

Instead, Daryl acts like I just told him I have a doctor's appointment this afternoon and I need to leave early.

This solidifies everything I knew within myself.

This job does not care about me. This company doesn't care about me.

A part of me wishes I had told Daryl to go to hell over the phone, and got on that plane with Landon, and figured out everything when I got home. Maybe everything would be different.

"Okay, well, I guess this is my resignation," I say.

Turning on my heel, I leave, and I cannot believe I just quit *my fucking job*.

Something my friends have been telling me to do for years.

Something Landon saw within four hours of being around me.

A huge boulder has lifted off my shoulders, and I feel light, buoyant in the air.

I collect my stuff, including my meager collection of

supplies I brought with me to the office, and I leave, feeling like Jerry Maguire—without the grand speeches. I am full of hope and optimism, and the anxious nerves flow away.

It doesn't hit me until I leave the building.

What did I just do?

Cassie is home when I walk in. She is busy setting up her camera facing a huge green screen. The noise-canceling curtains are already hung, thick black curtains made of heavy fabric that block light and most of the street sounds.

Cassie is an ASMR artist—a creator on YouTube who makes people sleep, essentially, usually by whispering or tapping on things. I thought it was a joke at first when she first started getting into it, but she now has over three hundred thousand subscribers on YouTube and gets sponsorship deals for one video that is more than I make in a month.

"Hey, girl. You're home early," Cassie says. "I'm about to film a video. Will you be around?"

"I just quit my job," I say, my voice cascading down.

"Holy shit, really?" Cassie covers her mouth in disbelief. "I can't believe you actually did it."

"I did," I say, flopping onto the couch. My bed set-up is folded at the end, and my head rests on the pillow stacked on top of the sheets. Now that my greatest stressor is gone, I could fall asleep and not wake up for five years.

Once Cassie starts her video, I may fall asleep and never wake up.

"Did you hear from that guy?" Cassie asks as she pulls a small desk over and props one of her microphones on top of it. I shake my head.

"You gave him your number, right?"

"No. I'm such an idiot. I let him go down on me."

"Hey, never apologize for getting your pussy licked," Cassie says, angling the microphone.

"I sucked his dick, too," I say.

"Well, it's only fair," Cassie replies.

"Maybe Landon was right. Maybe it was just a chance encounter. He isn't *the one* or anything."

"I'm okay with anything that gets you over that other loser," Cassie says. She refuses to say Patrick's name since he left me at the altar.

I bury my head in the pillows. "I'm more upset about Landon than my job."

"Wow," Cassie says. "I have to film several videos today. If you want to be on camera, I can do a hair-brushing video."

"No thanks," I say. "I think I will go walk around. Maybe get some coffee. So, you can film your videos."

"Thanks, love," Cassie says. She stands up and opens her arms. I walk into them. Her arms are tiny, but they give the best hugs, full and crushing. She separates with a smile. "Chin up. It's only up from here."

I smile, grabbing a pair of yoga pants and a white shirt. I change quickly and slip on my white sneakers. After I grab my phone and card and slip into my down jacket, I leave, and I'm outside.

I don't know where I'm going or what I'm doing. I just quit my job. I have no boyfriend, no real apartment. The wind is as aimless as I am.

My favorite place is the perfect solution—a coffee shop next to an independent bookstore—and I pop in. A distinct book smell hits my nostrils, and I close my eyes to focus on the smell. Books always give great comfort, no matter what stage of life you're in.

The line for the coffee counter is long, maybe six people deep.

All my problems will be temporarily solved by a soy latte.

I pull out my phone as I wait, standing behind a man with blond hair, wearing a flannel shirt.

Instagram sucks me in, and I scroll through photo after photo of a happy life veneer. What pain lurks behind those photos? Who is in a loveless marriage? Who can't pay their rent?

I'm so engrossed that I don't see the person in front of me turn around.

"Erin?"

I look up, and Landon Walcott, my rowmate and one-night, third-base stand, stands in front of me.

The shock on his face must match the one on mine.

8

"Hi," I eek out as a smile flirts on his lips.

"I hoped I would see you around," Landon says, looking around. He shoves his hands in his pockets and shifts back and forth on the balls of his feet.

I tuck my hair behind my ear. "You remembered."

"Barely," he says, looking at the ceiling and back at me. "I've been switching between multiple coffee shops that are connected to bookshops. I've been hanging out at City Lights too, just in case it was that one."

"Wow, you went all the way over there? Do you live around here?"

Landon shakes his head. His lips rub together with a gleaming eye.

There's so much to say.

"So, is this fate?" I ask. I honestly do not know how he will answer.

"I don't know," Landon says. "I just know that I can't stop thinking about you. I tried; I was skeptical. But from that first moment I saw you, something happened. It's never happened to me before."

He takes my hand in his and swings our closed fists between us, like we are crushes on the school playground. "I am so sorry I did not get your phone number."

"Why didn't you?" I ask.

"Let's go sit over there," he says with a point. We get out of line and walk to a crumb-covered black table in the corner. Landon wipes up the crumbs and throws them away like a gentleman.

He sits down and clasps his hands together. "I was raised by a single mother. She claims my dad was the love of her life, and she met him one night. One night. He disappeared, and she was *convinced* my no-good dad was it. We wasted a lot of years trying to find him, just to find out he had a wife and children and didn't care about us.

"When I met you, I had no idea that could happen. That you could be that connected after one night. You were this lightning bolt that hit me when I least expected it. I don't know what happened, but I knew. I *knew,* but I let you go."

He rubs his hair and locks eyes with me. "I've had girlfriends before. I always thought I had to build to some great relationship. It took work and sacrifice and time. Then, you came in, and I felt closer to you than I had ever felt to anyone. It threw me for a loop, you know."

I could cry right now. After all the men I've been with, men who weren't sure about me when we were about to get married, and I sat with a man who was sure about me after less than twenty-four hours.

"I remembered that you love coffee shops connected to bookstores. The freedom to get a coffee and then peruse without having to go outside. I needed to find you. I couldn't find you on social media..."

"I deleted Facebook, and my Instagram is super private. There is no way you could've found me," I add.

"Okay," Landon says. He grabs my hands again, and his eyes are like a claw that grabs my heart. "I am so sorry I thought what we had was nothing. It was something. It was a lot more than something."

He whips out his phone and unlocks it. "Erin Blank Campbell, may I have your phone number?"

"Yes," I say. I recite it to him, and he texts me.

There it is. Landon's phone number. I hold my phone to my chest like it's a treasure I thought long lost.

"Now, you have mine," he says.

"My middle name is Phyllis," I say, leaning forward. I blush, and he lets out a laugh.

"Phyllis? Like *The Office*? I love it!"

"It is after my great-aunt that my mom was close to. Supposedly, she was a riot."

"Erin Phyllis Campbell. That is such a good name."

"Thanks," I say.

He turns his phone around, and I'm in his phone as *Erin Phyllis Campbell.*

I follow suit and enter his name as *Landon Bernard Walcott.*

"I'm so glad I found you," he says. He shakes his head in disbelief. "It had to be fate. It had to be real. It was love at first sight—for me, anyway."

"It was. For me, too," I say. He kisses my hand, and it sends shivers up my arm.

We are quiet for a moment, and I say, "I quit my job today."

"Wow, really?" Landon stands up and attacks me with a bear hug. "I'm so proud of you."

"I could hear your voice in my head the entire time. My boss wasn't going to give me that promotion. He was just using it as a ploy to get me back to New York."

"I wondered about that," Landon says. "I think we should celebrate."

Worry about money must seep into my expression, because he adds, "On me."

"Okay," I say. He stands up and offers his hand. I take it, and I stand up.

We have a lovely evening and an even better night. We eat at a tiny restaurant that overlooks the water, and I feel at peace, like my life is locking into place. Everything before felt shaggy, out of control. Now, it feels like it has always been this way, and Landon has always been in my life.

We drink decent margaritas and watch the sun set. After we ride back to his place in a rideshare, I follow him into his apartment and meet Henry, who is sitting on the couch, holding a game controller.

"Hey, Henry, this is Erin," Landon says.

"Oh, so you're the mysterious lady," Henry says. "I knew all Landon needed was you."

That statement hits me, and I smile.

We are kissing before his bedroom door closes.

"I have condoms this time," he says, his breath hot on my cheek, and I pull his flannel off him.

"Oh really," I say.

"This apartment is much nicer than the motel room anyway."

This is the cleanest man's space I have ever seen. All manly dark blues and gray. Photos of him with an older woman, probably his mom, on his bookshelf. A diploma hangs over his desk.

My shirt comes off quickly and his is soon after.

He kisses me with the promise of a tomorrow, making me swell with a desire that calms the chaotic parts of me. It doesn't matter I am jobless or in between apartments. He was the catalyst, the starting point. Everything is before and after him.

When I step out of my leggings, standing there with my hips sticking out sharply, he looks at me like I'm the sexiest woman he has ever seen. He takes my face in his hands, and they travel from my ass to palm my breasts and to that in-between that screams for him—has been waiting for a man like him.

"Are you okay?" he asks as he lays me down on the bed, crouching so he's level with my sex. I nod with a plea, and he dives into me, flicking his tongue against the most sensitive part of me. I'm back in that dingy motel in Waterloo that is still one of the most erotic moments of my life, receiving and giving pleasure with a stranger that became so much more.

After he rolls a condom onto his length, he pushes into me, and liquid warmth whips within my core. He brings me to the brink again as he holds one leg up, thrusting into me like he has no finish line to cross. It's about this moment.

My leg drapes over his shoulder as he leans in to kiss my collarbone, my neck, and I cry out as the orgasm shatters me. He comes shortly after with a grunt so deep and settles into me.

"Henry heard every bit of that," I say with a laugh.

"Probably did. Henry is cool, though. He had to listen to me talk about you endlessly when I got home."

Landon slips out of me to dispose of the condom. I prop up on my elbow and watch him as he disappears into his en suite bathroom, an anomaly for most San Francisco apartments.

"What happens now?" I ask.

"The rest of our lives."

Usually, a statement like this would alarm me. If Patrick

would've said something like this to me after our official first date and the two, maybe third cumulative day we had together, I may have run, had drinks with the girls, and told them about this stalker guy I went on a date with.

Still, with Landon...it feels like fate.

It feels destined.

It feels meant to be.

EPILOGUE

"Are you ready?" Landon asks me as he slaps the boarding passes across his hands. He leans in for a quick peck that warms my insides.

"Ready," I say as we walk away from the Skyline Airlines counter toward security. I have spent so many minutes alone in the TSA lines, watching other couples and families excited to go on vacation with their loved ones.

I am now that person who has found my person.

To say he is my everything is so small, so tiny in comparison. I do not know now where he begins and I end.

He looks for ways to touch me—a brief brush of fingertips against my side, a graze of his short nails along my arms. He kisses my neck for no reason.

The anticipation for this trip was delicious; each day was one step closer, and the excitement built.

Thankfully, my love is doing well for himself. He sold the Kindred app for a pile of money. I came home one day to see him having a Scrooge McDuck moment, rolling around on our bed in a lot of filthy cash.

"Did you start dealing drugs?" I asked.

"I sold the app."

I ran toward him, and then we had sex on top of the money.

It sounds ridiculous and unsanitary, but it was *fun*.

To celebrate, he is taking me on a dream vacation, beginning in Barcelona and snaking down the Mediterranean. I am finally seeing the Santorini Islands.

A year has flown by since that fateful plane ride from New York to Waterloo, Iowa.

We got a tiny apartment together. I started working for a nonprofit that focuses on books and reading with impoverished youth. I make a sliver of my old salary, and while my bank account is meager on most days, my heart is full.

Landon jokes that he's my sugar daddy, and I am more than okay with it.

We haven't been on a plane ride since that day because Landon always wanted the next plane ride to be special, a milestone. He keeps saying this trip is to celebrate our meet-anniversary and selling the app, but I think he may propose to me on this trip. We picked out a ring two months ago, and I know he has it somewhere.

We weave in and out of the airport stores, collecting snacks and entertainment. I purchase a new thriller I've had my eye on and a Diet Coke while Landon can't decide on a magazine. When he looks across the brightly colored airport store at me, my heart still skips a beat.

We hold hands as we wait in chairs for our flight to be called.

Landon bounces his leg nervously as we wait.

"Are you nervous?" I ask.

"Yes. You remember, taking off makes me nervous. Also, what if I have to go to the bathroom and I get stuck?"

I laugh, remembering screaming to have someone let me out—Jade, the flight attendant, coming to my rescue.

"Or a dog gets loose?"

"Or a man takes off his shoes to air out his nasty-ass feet?"

"And then you get into a fight with him."

"Well, that plane ride was perfect—since I met you." Landon takes my hand and kisses it, and I melt.

"Do you now believe in fate?"

"Fate. Love at first sight. All of it."

The plane is announced, and we get in line. We board, and we have a middle and aisle seat again, but Landon lets me sit on the aisle.

"Oh fuck, I forgot something," Landon says. "I have to get off this plane."

"What did you forget?" I ask, so confused. He disappears, and I look for him. All the passengers are seated, ready for takeoff.

Where is Landon?

The plane intercom comes on. "Ladies and gentlemen, this is your captain speaking. We have a special surprise for the passenger in 34C."

Everyone checks their seat number, even those to the front of the plane.

I look up as well, and holy shit, I'm 34C.

It's happening now.

Then, my darling boyfriend appears with the radio to his mouth.

"I didn't believe in fate or love at first sight. Then I met you. I fought it. I agonized over it. When you left me in Iowa, I felt a deep hole in my heart that I had never felt before— with anyone. You were what was missing. You are more than my everything. I love you, and I've loved you since that time you caught my fake tooth in your hand."

Landon walks down the aisle as ladies ooh and aaw, and multiple heads turn to watch him walk toward me. My eyes are already misty as Landon takes my hand and drops to one knee.

"Erin Phyllis Campbell, I love you. Marry me. Go on a million more airplane rides with me. Anywhere I go with you is an adventure."

Tears come to my eyes, and I'm overcome.

All I can do is nod and kiss him. Tears stream down my face.

I kiss him, my forever rowmate.

Every misstep, every broken promise led me to Landon.

I feel happy.

I feel loved.

I feel grounded enough that I can soar.

The entire plane erupts into applause as Landon kisses me deeply.

"This is your captain speaking. We are about to take off. If you are standing, including the gentleman who just proposed, please be seated."

Landon sits down next to me, and it's perfect.

THE END

BONUS: WHEN ERIN LEFT

LANDON

I didn't ask for her phone number.

There's been some epically dumb things I've done over my lifetime, but that has to be numero uno.

Ex-girlfriends have broken up with me, saying my heart is cold. I'm unfeeling. I must've missed the day in school that taught sentimentality. My gregariousness throws people off constantly. In high school, I was named Most Likely to Chat Up a Stranger. My business partner and roommate, Henry, has pushed me in front of crowds to give work speeches because everyone, including our PR manager, calls me *charming*. It's always felt like a skin I wear, something I put on like a pair of pants. When you peel back the jokes and the friendliness, all you see is stone.

But Erin no-middle-name Campbell. I forget sometimes about the multiple zeroes in my bank account, booking coach out of habit. That's how I ended up next to her, in an aisle seat. Over the course of our flight, I watched her come to life, like Cinderella once she's hit with the Fairy Godmother's wand. It was us, our connection.

We spent one beautiful night in a questionably clean Waterloo hotel and now she's gone.

She left and now I'm standing in this tiny Iowa airport, frozen in place. Her hair, the color of espresso, swung as she walked toward her gate. I thought she'd look back, but she didn't and then she was gone. I let her go without getting her phone number. Because I'm an idiot.

The flight home from Iowa to San Francisco is a blur. I spent the almost four hours, staring at the little cartoon plane on our personal monitor, moving a half a centimeter over an imaginary line of dashes and dots. If I focused, I could remember how her hand felt in mine, how her strawberry-red lips tasted, how her skin scorched my palms when I ran them against her.

She conceded to my thoughts on fate, how I don't believe in it, but I could tell she was lying. She believed in all of that, that we were meant to meet each other, that we were destined. The invisible string theory. How we could've passed each other in a San Francisco Trader Joe's, time after time, until fate pushed us together on a flight.

Before Erin, I didn't think fate was a thing. Life is a bunch of coincidences and then you die.

However, this flight wasn't any flight. It was the kind of flight you talk about in the nursing home when you're ninety. A girl you talk about with affection even decades later, when your grandson falls in love for the first time.

When I exit SFO in a daze, I miraculously find my car in the parking garage. I drive home and park, and when I walk into the apartment, I find Henry, reading a book on the couch.

"There you are," Henry says. While I need to book first class tickets with my money, my best friend could stand to buy new clothes. There's a hole in his collar and he's wearing those dingy black socks again.

"How was it?" he asks.

"Well, they made us an offer." I tell Henry what it was and his eyes bulge. "What did Harvey say?"

"Harvey thinks he can get twenty percent more. Said I would talk to you. Thanks for keeping your cell phone by you, by the way."

"Hey, I was deep in my creativity." Henry's eyes squint. I peer at the book in his lap. He's reading Ray Bradbury. Again.

"Well, next time, keep it near you." My tone is harsh, and Henry shakes his head.

"Spill."

What?"

"Spill. You're mad about something. Is it the deal?"

"No, I..." If I tell someone else about it, it's real. It meant something. Unlike what I told her. Add that to the list of regrets. I made Erin feel like she didn't mean everything. "I didn't get a lot of sleep. I met a girl. On the flight."

"What? You?"

All Henry has seen of my plane behavior is oversized headphones, neck pillow, eye mask and lights out. Sometimes, the only people I talk to on the flights are the flight attendants to thank them.

"She was...just...special."

"Um-hum," Henry says, as his eyes focus on his book.

I think he's let it go, but after he flips a page, he says, "Where is she from?"

"Here. She lives with a roommate."

"Oh. So, are you going to see her again?"

I squirm although I'm standing, my luggage still in my hand. "I don't think so."

Henry shuts his book with a thwack and I drop my suitcase I'm so startled. "What?"

"You thought it was nothing, so you didn't get her phone number, did you?"

I've known Henry for a shorter time than most of my best friends, but Henry can see through me like I'm cheesecloth. "I didn't. I just thought it was a fluke on an airplane. All this weird stuff happened. There was a chihuahua that got loose, and I found it and I got punched..." I show Henry my empty space where my fake tooth came loose. My fake tooth is currently with my toiletries.

"You didn't think this girl was weird too? Like out of the ordinary? It would be one thing if it was a normal flight and you met her, but all that stuff... You got stuck in Iowa, bro."

"I know." I rub my hand down my face.

"Did anything happen?"

My mouth crooks. Erin looked so beautiful laid out on the motel bedspread as I parted her legs and tasted her. How it felt to be in her mouth as she worked her magic, making me come harder than I had ever had. How could I deny this was a run-of-the-mill encounter? Everything pointed to Erin being special. And I botched it.

"You hussy. So what, you're going to see if you run into each other and make it a coincidence?"

"No," I say. Now my hand rakes my hair. My skin feels like it's crawling, like I'm still uncomfortable, even though I'm in my swanky San Francisco apartment with the business partner who ushers spiders out of our house like they deserve respect.

"Well, I think you should do something about it." Henry turns to me, his face as serious as a heart attack. "I feel like you're going to spend a good chunk of time regretting not making an effort to find her."

I DON'T SLEEP that night. Or the night after. Every time I close my eyes, I think about her. The regret eats at me, consuming my waking thoughts. We talk with our attorney and make a counteroffer, hoping it'll stick. The company who wants to buy our app will take care of our little tech baby, and we can move onto the next thing, the next project. We have a list of ideas and Henry's built enough model airplanes to fill a corner of our apartment. It's time for us to get to work again.

The third night, I toss and turn, every spot of my bed gouging me. The clock glows with 2:37 and I do the math. I've been uncomfortable for three hours and it's because of her. My self-hatred for my self-preservation.

I grope for my phone and open Facebook. Nothing for Erin Campbell. On Instagram, I find some users with that name, but none of the avatars are that woman who is consuming my thoughts. I think about cold DMing—*Hi are you the woman I can't stop thinking about that I met on Skyline Flight # ----? Because I should've gotten your phone number, but I didn't.*

I throw my phone onto my head and rub my forehead. *Think, Landon, think.* I go through all the facts. She didn't mention her company but there's a million investment firms or the like in the city. That's a baby needle in a football stadium filled with hay. Her roommate does ASMR on YouTube; maybe I can find her that way.

Typing ASMR into the YouTube search engine gives me listing after listing. After three pages I don't see anything getting me closer to her. Erin's not the subject of any video and I slam my laptop shut.

Why didn't I remember to ask for her phone number again?

Erin talked about fate, that we were meant to meet each other. I downplayed it, made her feel like she wasn't special. That I hadn't felt that alive in a long time, sitting next to her on a flight. How touching her, kissing her turned me into the best version of myself. I liked what she brought out of me, and I let her go.

Dad issues follows you for a lifetime, I guess.

My mom romanticized her relationship with my dad for years. I was conceived after one night of passion and she *knew* if she found him and told him, we would be a family. *It was magical, meeting your father,* she would tell me, as a ten-year-old eating Lucky Charms on a random Thursday morning. She hired a private investigator just to find my dad fifteen years into a marriage with a woman named Rita, with two children-- one in middle school, one in high school. That's when I realized my mom's rosy memory was a lie.

My dad cheated on his wife with my mother. While my mother had spent every day thinking about him, he didn't give her a second thought.

That's why I didn't get Erin's phone number. It's why every girlfriend rolled her eyes when she broke up with me. They knew I wasn't into it as much as they were and they saved themselves, put themselves first. *I wish you were more sentimental*, my ex Taryn told me as she collected her items from around my apartment to leave.

I was so scared to be a fool like my mom that I didn't go after a woman in an airport. A woman I knew deep down was different. Someone my heart pounded around, who made me want to be better. Get over my shit for her. She's not my dad.

She's ten times the person he is.

Then, it comes to me. *I love coffee shops attached to bookstores. If I have a weekend afternoon, I get a latte and peruse the shelves. I could be there for hours.*

That's when I reopened my laptop and typed in "bookstores with coffee shops, san Francisco, ca". After finding my phone, I started listing bookstores to visit, to get a glimpse of her. I would search high and low, looking for her. If I saw her again, I would give fate a try. Maybe see it from her perspective.

I spend all weekend, oscillating through all the likely options. We get word from Harvey late Saturday night that he got us our twenty percent and we verbally told him, yes. Let's sell.

Something told me to go that Monday. I wasn't sure what, but I stood in line for a double shot of espresso just to feel a prickle at the back of my neck. My heart lurches when I turn and she's here. She's not a dream, or a vision. My intuition told me to come this weekday and she's here.

"Erin?" I ask.

When she looks up, her eyes widen when she sees me, and a small smile crosses those lips I've dreamt about for days.

"Hi," she says, and it hits me like a kick to the stomach.

The universe wants me to be with her. I was just too stubborn to notice.

In Case of Emergency

1

———

We're in the lobby of the Octavo only five seconds before we see him.

"Oh no," Nessa says, with a point. "Um, Cassie?"

I freeze and scan. My "cocky bastard" radar has been pricked. "Where is *he*?"

"Over there," Nessa says.

Fury bubbles under my skin.

Smith Kennedy. My former boss and the biggest asshole I've ever met guards the elevators like a sexy gargoyle.

I suffered for five years under Mr. Kennedy as his legal assistant. Underappreciated, dismissed. The last time I saw him, he yelled at me from across his mahogany desk and I quit on the spot. It's been nine months, but I still feel the potent cocktail of pissed and hurt from the day I quit.

It would be easier if he wasn't so damn good-looking.

He's looking down at his phone, leaning against a wall. His black suit skims his body too perfectly, and his signature graying hair is styled like a Ken doll's.

"I thought he wasn't coming," I say, pulling Nessa in the

bathroom. A deep sigh of relief exits my lips as I'm safe in the ladies'.

"I thought he wasn't either. I didn't see him at the ceremony," Nessa says. "Mr. Jones is his best friend so it makes sense. Still, sucks for you."

"Totally," I agree.

I was nervous for three days leading up to this wedding, but Nessa assured me there was a good chance he wouldn't show. Plus, I had to show up for my friend, my gay work husband, Vincent. He and Quentin Jones, one of the other partners in the law firm, fell in love when Vincent was in the legal assistant trenches with me two years ago. When it looked like it was getting serious, Vincent graciously resigned and found a position with a personal injury firm. He offered to slip my resume in when I quit, but I declined.

If all attorneys treated me the way Mr. Kennedy did, I was done with my legal career.

When I still worked at Froman, Jones, and Kennedy, Vincent would patiently and quietly listen to me rant about Mr. Kennedy at brunch, letting me describe in detail the latest thing he did to crumble my cookies.

The week before I quit, Vincent stopped me, mid-rant.

"Are you sure you hate him?" Vincent would ask, pouring more champagne. "Hate sex could be fun."

"He's married," I said, confused that was my first objection. Not that he was my boss, not that I seethed every time I saw him.

"Yeah, well," Vincent would say, drinking his mimosa in a suspicious way.

"Even if he was single, it would never work. He's the worst," I said.

"Uh-huh," Vincent said.

My hatred of Smith Kennedy reached an epic proportion when he pulled me into his office the day I quit. I hadn't even had my coffee yet.

"I have a mediation today?" Mr. Kennedy asked.

I opened my work phone to his calendar. I nodded once.

"Then why the fuck was no call scheduled with the client?" Mr. Kennedy seethed. He paced behind his desk, running his fingers through his hair. "We're going to go into it with no communication with the client, no authority to settle and we'll look like fucking idiots. You know this plaintiff attorney is a giant pain in my ass. Is the client even going to be present?"

Like I always did, I switched to problem-solving mode, scrolling through his calendar, wondering how I'd messed up so badly. I *never* messed up. Then, I remembered those three days another legal assistant, Mandy, watched my desk while I went to a bachelorette party in Lake Tahoe.

"Mandy must've overlooked it when she was covering my desk," I said. "I'm so sorry. I can get the client on the phone right now. I can salvage this."

Mr. Kennedy's cuff links glittered as he jabbed his finger at me. "Don't blame the girl *you* trained. You fucked this up. How could you? I trust you to handle my calendar, and I can't trust you anymore. Don't you see that?"

His voice raised, and he slammed his fist to the desk.

In the moment, I was frozen, my mouth hung open. Days later, I thought of a million things I could've said. How he was the attorney and could watch his own calendar, schedule his own pre-mediation conference, and how it was good client care. How I gave the firm five years of my life, stayed late, smoothed over clients, settled deals for him, all without an ounce of appreciation of my efforts. How this was my first mistake ever in the whole time I'd been working as his assistant.

He never talked to me, but now that I overlooked something, he yelled at me.

I could feel a sob behind my eyes, but I held it together. I spent five years *hating* my job, *hating* my boss, and this was the final straw. I was done.

"You know what?" I said, standing up. "I quit."

He looked stunned. "Cassie, please," he said. His use of my nickname startled me. He always called me Ms. Gallagher or Cassandra, never Cassie. It felt intimate and confusing to hear it from a man I hated, who didn't even know my birthday.

Crying started the minute I left with my cardboard box of things, walking down Sacramento Street. Even the homeless people who sometimes blocked my path looking for spare change let me be. The last five years of my life reduced to a flimsy box full of my snarky coffee mugs and a picture of me with my best friends, Sarah and Erin.

All because I let an asshole man get to me. Something I swore I was done doing.

I also said I wouldn't cower in shame in bathrooms anymore, but here I am again.

Nessa studies me. "You're really red. Are you sure you're okay?"

I look up at the mirror to my reflection, sweaty, my angry cheeks overpowering my light pink blush.

Nessa flares her nostrils and covers her face. "You might want to refresh your deodorant, honey. You're ripe."

"I am?" I ask, lifting my armpit to sniff. She is absolutely right.

It's all Mr. Kennedy's fault. That man makes me sweat-rage.

"It will all be fine," Nessa comforts, placing a hand on my shoulder. Her round brown eyes are concerned as she watches me go through bad memories of working for him. Wonder how I'm going to get through this night being in the same room.

"I'm fine. I can survive one night. He won't even talk to me anyway," I say. I've hated people before, but it was always linked to a healthy dose of ambivalence. I usually forget about people I hate, but I haven't been able to forget Smith Kennedy.

I don't know what that means and it bugs me.

"Let's go back out there," I say. Nessa follows me as we exit the bathroom and sneak to the corner.

Mr. Kennedy is still pacing the perimeter, acknowledging people with a dismissive head nod.

"Did he get better-looking?" I ask.

"Smith has always looked that good," Nessa says.

"Oh my God, Cassie!" Arlene, another former co-worker, yells when she sees me, and I shush her in response. After she takes me in a bone-crushing hug, Arlene lowers her voice. "Am I supposed to whisper?"

"Mr. Kennedy is over there," Nessa whispers, and Arlene joins us around the corner. Arlene sat directly across from me in a cubicle as a fellow legal assistant. She's saved my ass more than once, interpreting Spanish statements and emails and accompanied me to a crying episode in the bathroom numerous times. A good twenty years older than me, Arlene joined Nessa and Vincent as the best parts of Froman, Jones, and Kennedy.

"He's disgusting," I say.

Arlene and Nessa stare at me, their eyes calling me out on my bullshit.

Mr. Kennedy is the opposite of disgusting and we all know it. Objectively handsome, he's six-three, with broad shoulders and a tapered waist. He must have his tailor on retainer since his pants and shirts are always perfectly fitted.

Days-old scruff constantly shadows his jaw, his full lips always pursed in disapproval. His graying hair adds to his sexiness, although he's only in his early forties. He is a full twelve years older than me, but I knew if I saw him on a dating app without knowing what I know, I would definitely swipe right.

I've always had a thing for older men. The more broken, the better.

My taste is why I'm taking an indefinite break from anyone with a penis.

"Why aren't you going up to the reception?" Arlene asks.

"He's blocking the elevators," I say. "Is he waiting for Daniela or something?"

Nessa and Arlene look at each other before looking at me.

"What?"

"Mr. Kennedy got divorced. He announced it about three months after you left," Arlene says.

I gasp. Then, I'm smiling. Wait, why am I smiling?

His misery is my joy. That's it.

"What happened?" I ask, leaning in.

"Well," Arlene says, leaning in closer. Nessa also leans in, turning her head to hear better. "Daniela left him."

My mouth breaks into a grin.

"Um-hum, that's what I heard too," Nessa says. "Poof, she was gone. Vincent saw her out once, and she's already with a new man. Mr. Kennedy looked so sad for months."

"I wonder why Vincent didn't tell me." I thought we were besties. Shaking my head, I lean in. "Do you know why they broke up?"

"I think someone cheated," Arlene whispers. "No one knows which one for sure."

I've met Mr. Kennedy's now ex-wife, Daniela a handful of times. Her olive skin always glowed, and she created her own wind as she glided between the cubicles. Born in Venezuela, she came to the States and met Mr. Kennedy when he was in law school and she was a cocktail waitress at Everdene, a rooftop bar in the Virgin hotel. They always looked so good together. I didn't know there was trouble in paradise.

"It had to be his fault," I whisper. "Because men are trash."

"Oh honey, has it been a while?" Nessa's patronizing arm wraps around my shoulders, and I roll my eyes.

"I'm happily single," I say. *Although I do miss sex. Badly.*

As of this month, I have been single for three glorious years. My wakeup call was when my last boyfriend cheated on me with a woman who attended protests, no matter the topic. He was the last in a long line of cheaters, ghosts, and gaslighters and I had had enough.

The easy answer is no-strings-attached, casual sex, but there's nothing casual about me. The minute a man looks at me, I catch feelings and I know I can slip back to where I was three years ago.

Chasing men who don't want me.

The side of Nessa's mouth quirks. "If you decide to get back out there, I'm sure you can find an admirer from your YouTube comments."

I roll my eyes. My YouTube channel, Cassie Whispers, has blown up, and I now make a full-time income off of my sponsorships and ad revenue, doing ASMR videos. ASMR stands for autonomous sensory meridian response, a type of sensation that is deeply relaxing or causes tingles in some people.

It was crazy how fast my channel grew, with its impulsive beginnings. One night after three days of unemployment and too many glasses of Pinot Grigio, I filmed a video and uploaded it. The channel is the whole reason I can still afford my stupidly expensive apartment in the city. Being a YouTuber comes with its own sets of challenges, though. Like men offering ten thousand dollars for a pair of my used underwear in the DMs.

Vincent talked me out of saying yes.

"That girlfriend video, talk about a thirst trap," Nessa says. "I was almost asleep when my husband came in and asked me what I was watching.'"

The video of my latest roleplay, "Your Girlfriend Soothes You to Sleep," has already gotten over three hundred thousand views. I had to turn off the comments. Too many men requesting to smell my hair.

"It's a sultry video, Cassie," Arlene says. "I was even blushing."

Nessa grabs me around my shoulders and loudly says, "Our own Cassie Gallagher, YouTube star. With over five hundred thousand subscribers!"

"Keep your voice down," I say. Mr. Kennedy still hovers in front of the elevators, looking around. "And it's seven hundred thousand fifty-two. As of this morning."

Nessa grabs my arm. "This is stupid. We should politely say hi, go up to the reception, and then avoid him. With cocktails."

"Fine," I say as I step closer to Arlene. She says nothing but reaches into her purse and hands me a stick of deodorant. I should be embarrassed, but I'm just grateful.

"Arlene and I will make sure Mr. Kennedy isn't blocking the elevator. Go freshen up," Nessa says.

They leave me, and I go into the bathroom again, use Arlene's deodorant, and drop it into my purse.

"You can do this," I tell myself in the mirror.

"You *can* do this," a woman from a stall yells. "I believe in you!"

"Thanks!" A stranger's comment will fuel my perseverance through this night. The best support I've received from other women *always* happens in bathrooms.

As I walk into the lobby, I catch movement in my peripheral vision. I turn to see my nemesis, the face I see when I take kickboxing classes with Erin. Mr. Kennedy, his eyes looking everywhere but at me, bobbing on the balls of his feet.

His left hand free of his expensive platinum band.

Looking way too sexy for how vile his personality is.

"Hi," he says, his voice like sandpaper. His eyes look anywhere but at mine.

"Hello, Mr. Kennedy," I choke out the words.

I cross my arms and stare straight at him. This is my chance to say everything from my revenge fantasies. My golden ticket.

He's not my boss anymore. He's just an asshole in a really nice suit.

His lips part, a brief escape of air audible. Are his eyes actually blue? Did my bosom just heave?

This is bad. Really bad.

"Gotta go," I say. I run for the elevator. I press the up button like my life depends on it.

The doors open, and I tumble in, out of breath from running twenty feet. God, I need to hit the gym more often.

I'm sweating again as I wait for an arm with a muscular

forearm to stop it. The doors close, and I let out a long sigh. I'm free. I have escaped.

Then the doors open again.

Son of a bitch.

Smith looks up, fixing a cufflink like a model in a men's wear commercial.

He steps in.

"We really need to talk."

2

"No, we don't," I say, stabbing the button for the fifteenth floor.

Only fifteen floors and I can be at this wedding and can avoid him the rest of the night.

I wedge myself in the sharp corner of the elevator car as it climbs. I've had Brazilian waxes more comfortable than this.

Mr. Kennedy shoves his hands in his pockets and looks to the ground.

Suddenly, the elevator jerks and then stills.

Did it just stop?

The doors remain closed, and I look up at the number, which flickers between a four and a five.

Are we...stuck?

"How are you?" he asks, completely oblivious to our situation.

Oh, for the love of pig shit. Seriously? He wants to make small talk when I'm pretty sure this elevator has stopped working?

"I'm great, thanks for asking. Are we moving?" I ask, a

touch of panic in my voice. My hands press against the sides. The elevator shifts slightly.

"I'm...not sure."

We both stare at the number, hoping our brain waves will move this elevator.

No such luck.

We are, for sure, stuck.

This is literally my worst nightmare.

You don't think you're claustrophobic until you're stuck in a small space with the worst boss you've ever had. A boss who just happens to be hot, and you've spent years denying that your body hums every time he gets within feet of you.

Mr. Kennedy reaches for the open door button and tries it.

Nothing happens.

"This is not good," I say.

"No shit," he says calmly, punching every button like Buddy the Elf with no results. The doors open a few inches, then freeze. No way either of us could squeeze our three-dimensional bodies through.

He steps back, hands on his hips.

"Well, this is not promising."

"No shit," I serve back. "We're stuck."

"We're not stuck. Just momentarily stagnant."

Mr. Kennedy moves around, calm as a bomb defusal technician, trying the buttons, trying to open the doors while I stand in the corner, unable to move.

"Some help would be appreciated," he says. "We should try to open the doors."

"I asked my neighbor to carry a watermelon for me the other day. I'm not your girl."

"Fine. I guess there's a reason I pay for my trainer."

Mr. Kennedy takes off his suit jacket, and a tiny gasp

leaves my mouth. His shoulders are so broad, the muscles straining against the fabric...

No. I stare at the ceiling. The panels look movable. Will I have to crawl out of that like a blonde John McClane? Mr. Kennedy will have to hoist me up, so nope. I can't have him touching me, even if it would be really cool to climb through an air duct.

Mr. Kennedy takes his big hands and tries to pry the doors open and I watch like the weak woman I am. My head tilts as I study his triceps bulging against his shirt. His grunts transport me to an unwanted fantasy, him over me, moving in and out of me as I writhe in pleasure. I can see the shadows and crevices of his back muscles, defined and sinewy, and that ass in those pants...

Cassie, stop objectifying this terrible man.

I sincerely apologize to my gender for my lack of help in this situation and the fact I can't stop staring at his arms.

"Mr. Kennedy, I don't think it's working," I say.

"Please. Call me Smith," he says, stepping away, out of breath with a light sheen of sweat on his brow.

"Smith," I repeat, the word foreign and intimate on my tongue.

Heat swirls in my core, and I cross my legs like a high-end nineties model.

"What are we going to do?" I whine.

"I think we're stuck, Ms. Gallagher," Smith says, turning around. "There, I said it. Stuck. Do you have your phone?"

I fumble with my purse and pull out my device. My hand is shaking so much, I almost drop it.

I try to text. I try to call Nessa. Nothing.

I hold it up. "No service."

"Perfect," he says, rolling one sleeve up.

Good God, his forearms. I shake my head. He pulls his

own phone out of his pocket and checks. "I got nothing either."

He stands there, inactive. Has he given up?

It's up to me; I'm my only hope. I summon every spiteful bone in my body, because only my wound-tight, no-sex-in-three-years, vengeful ass can get us out of this fucking death trap.

"Out of my way," I say, exploding from my safe corner.

Smith steps back, giving me space to try everything he did.

I stab the open and close buttons like a middle-schooler at a crosswalk. While I can barely do a low-impact Pilates class without feeling like I was hit by a bus the next day, I still try to pry the doors open. My heels slide against the slick floor as I try to find leverage.

"It's not working, Ms. Gallagher."

"Call me Cassie." *Like you did after I quit. Say it like you wanted to bend me over the desk.*

Oh my God, what is wrong with me? *I hate him, I hate him, I hate him.*

A light sweat breaks out across my forehead, joining the dark moons of armpit sweat on the silk of my dress.

My panic has reached an eleven.

"Fuck...this...shit," I say, taking the chain of my purse and beating the door with my bag. A loud guttural scream comes from the depths of me, fueled by five years of work dissatisfaction.

"I...cannot...be...stuck...in....here....with...him."

When my voice has grown hoarse, when I have *calmed down*, I turn around to see Smith standing there. His steely eyes fix on me and I crumble in his stare.

"Are you done?" he asks.

My mouth gapes open.

"Everything will be fine. We need to hit the button with the bell. Can you do that for me, Cassie?"

His tone is patronizing, infuriating. Why didn't *he* hit the bell button?

Also, my name on his lips destroys me again.

No matter how rude he was to me, no matter how much he ignored me, no matter that he *yelled* at me, I will always rise and pledge allegiance to the dumb bitch anthem with my whole heart.

Instead, I stand there and cross my arms. Smith's eyes roll hard as he reaches around me, his arm inches from my breasts, to press the button himself. I hold a breath. He glares at me as he hits the In Case of Emergency button.

"We're in this together," he says. "You don't have to act like such a brat."

I fire back. "Let's not start on who the bigger brat is, *Smith*."

"Look, I'm not happy either. Being stuck in an elevator is not ideal," Smith says.

"With me, you mean."

His square jaw grinds, his lips rubbing together. Damn, those lips. I've never seen a better pair of lips wasted on a man whose personality didn't deserve them.

"I'm not a fan of being trapped. However, I do not regret being stuck with you. Seeing you scream was *very* entertaining."

"You are insufferable." I fume as the corner of his lip flick to a smirk.

"Why are you smiling like that?"

"Like what?" His lips break to a full-teeth, mocking smile.

"I will not engage. I will remain classy and in control of my volitions," I say to myself.

"What?" he asks, that cocky grin still there. His eyes, all sparkling and happy, clearly delight in my useless mantras. "You've always made me laugh."

"I'm glad my distress is amusing you." I could never hide emotions well, so Smith definitely picks up on the disgust on my face.

Smith crosses his arms, still smiling. "Oh, I knew it. You hate me."

Non-catastrophe Cassie would politely deny it. Catastrophe Cassie has no filter.

"I hate you because you hate me," I retort. My thumb bludgeons the call button so aggressively it hurts. "Why are they not answering the call button?"

"Well, it's good to see you have some fight in you. Reminds me of the woman who worked for me."

"You're lucky I'm not in the mood to go to jail tonight," I threaten. The intercom saves me from a criminal record.

"Uh, hello?" the voice from the intercom asks.

"Hi, we're stuck in the elevator. I think between the fourth and fifth floor. Can you get us out?" I ask.

"Oh, okay," the voice says. "Are there any medical emergencies?"

Thank God I didn't murder Smith and have to deal with the blood. "No, we're fine."

The intercom crackles to silence.

I look back at Smith, and he shakes his head at me. "You are handling it beautifully. I'll just watch."

I fume as my eyes dart from the doors to the intercom. I slap the elevator for emphasis, but damn that really hurt. "Where did he go?"

I start pacing. I jump up and down, which was a mistake. My heels are killing my feet just by standing.

"What if the cord breaks and we plunge to our death

because you're jumping like that?" he asks, folding his arms. He leans against the wall, next to an advertisement for the restaurant on the ground floor.

"That's not funny," I say in horror, pointing a finger.

"I think it's hilarious."

I roll my eyes.

The intercom crackles to life again, and I stand directly in front of it.

"So, I called the elevator technician, and he said it will be an hour and a half."

"An hour and a half?" I ask. "An hour and a *half*?"

"Yes, ma'am," the voice says. "It's Saturday night in San Francisco."

"I know that," I say. "Can't you call someone else?"

"I'm sorry, ma'am. We'll get you out of there as soon as possible."

I stamp my feet like I'm five.

A loud gurgle fills the elevator. My head snaps in Smith's direction.

"What was that?"

"My stomach," Smith says.

"Tell your stomach to pipe down, Mr. Kennedy."

"Seriously, call me Smith. We worked together long enough."

Until you yelled at me.

"What kind of name is Smith, anyway? You already sound like a law firm."

"Absolutely," he says. "Smith Cooper Kennedy. My destiny secured."

"Of course that's your name."

The intercom switches on.

"We'll get you out of there as soon as possible, ma'am,"

the voice says. There is a pause, but the intercom still buzzes with energy. "We're really sorry about this."

Then, the voice is gone, and the silence wraps around us like a poisonous vapor.

I slide to the ground. The fight has left my body.

I am stuck in an elevator with Smith Kennedy. Oh excuse me, Smith Cooper Kennedy. The man smug enough to have a law firm for a name when his name is literally part of a law firm.

I almost cry for the seventh time today, but I shake my head. No, we've made it five years of not crying in front of this cocky salt-and-pepper-haired asshole. He doesn't deserve my tears.

Especially when I only cry at animal shelter commercials. Those dogs deserve every bit of liquid from me. This man does not.

Closing my eyes centers me, and when I open them again, Smith is sitting as well, one leg bent, his other leg out straight. His suit jacket is draped over the handrail.

I unstrap my shoes. If we're going to be here for a while, might as well get comfortable.

"Are you ready to talk now?" Smith asks.

"Sure," I say. My eyes close again. If I don't look at him, maybe it will be easier.

"I'm really unsettled with the way things ended," Smith says. "Between us."

It sounds like we ended a relationship, not that I quit as his employee. Smith, all gruff and no-nonsense, sounds soft and vulnerable. I'm so confused.

My eyes snap open. "It was nine months ago. It's all worked out. I have a very successful YouTube channel. People appreciate me there. I get hundreds of emails saying

I cured their insomnia, that they can relax with my videos when they usually can't otherwise..."

"I know," he says. My eyes narrow on him. Has he watched my videos?

"You don't watch ASMR," I say with a laugh. "That's what my videos are. I'm sure you've never heard of it."

"Oh, I have. I watch ASMR videos every night. I'm highly receptive to the response. Also, it knocks me right out."

"Huh," I say. He definitely comes off as someone who would make fun of it or not understand it.

I'll give him a half point for that. But he's still terrible.

"I've actually watched some of yours," he says.

My head balloons with anxiety. I feel naked, exposed. "Oh, really. What do you think?"

He shrugs.

Aaaand his half point is taken away.

"I'm proud of you, though," he says.

My jaw drops. I've never heard him say those words.

God, he is such a dick.

"Why did you never say nice things like that to me at work?"

Smith looks away quickly. The gears turn in his head. "Let's not talk about that."

"Well, you brought it up."

"Let's talk about something else," he says, staring off to the corner.

I roll my eyes as I sift through all my typical getting-to-know-you questions. "Favorite TV show?"

"*Buffy the Vampire Slayer*," he says without skipping a beat.

Excuse me, what?

3

I love *Buffy the Vampire Slayer*. As an unmonitored eight-year-old, I watched it religiously and was convinced I would be called upon to be a slayer. I asked my mother for heeled boots and held long pieces of bark like a stake. I used to dedicate time every morning to practice my vampire slayer moves.

Buffy's influence even followed me to adulthood. It's why I have three pierced holes in my right ear and two in my left. It's why I wear gray polish too much and I've always been open to a *large* age gap with a partner.

It's why I'm snarky.

Now this man I detest holds the same affection for the best paranormal TV show ever made. Excuse me, best show ever made, period.

"I'm shocked," I say.

"Yeah, well," Smith says, standing up and folding his arms. His triceps pop against his white shirt, and I swallow... hard. "That program was revolutionary, and the comedy writing is some of the best of its time."

He's pacing now, like I paced earlier. Is it nerves?

"It's not weird," he says, nervous of my reaction.

"I have an important question," I say. He turns, his face pale. "Angel or Spike?"

His shoulders relax. "Angel, without a doubt," Smith says. "I also watched his show. When I say I'm a fan of that whole world, I meant I may or may not have been to a Comic-Con wearing a long trench coat."

Smith, my cool and collected former boss, went to Comic-Con. He cosplayed at Comic-Con.

"Did you have fangs?" I ask. He turns to me with an icy stare.

Oh, he totally has that shit.

"That's so...nerdy," I say.

Smith's pale cheeks collect red. His eyes do not look at mine as he says, "That show kept me company when I went away to college. I used to tape it on VHS in my dorm room and watch them when I got lonely. Fandoms give people more than you know. It gives people a sense of connection and community."

Smith's fists clench while his resolve crumbles. This man, who I thought had no feelings, whatsoever, is a sensitive dork underneath it all.

A dork who owns fangs and a trench coat.

That...is so hot.

I've never been into roleplaying, but I totally could get into some Angel and Buffy scenarios.

I've also never been into biting, but damn, I could get into that, too.

Smith sits down again in a huff, his arms draped across his knees. I scoot closer to him so our backs are pressed against the same wall.

I knock his shoulder with mine, a split decision I

instantly regret. The touch sends tingles down my arms, more than any ASMR video could.

"Confession time," I say. "I used to watch it, too."

"Oh yeah?" he says and he pauses. "Do I want to know how old you were when it was airing?"

I laugh. "I remember getting into it in first grade."

"Jesus," he says. "How old *are* you?"

"Thirty," I say. "You?" I already know, but he doesn't need to know that.

He chuckles, looking away. "Much older than that."

"I just thought the gray hair was from being an attorney."

"I wish," he says. "My dad went white at forty-eight. I'm not quite there yet, but it's going to happen."

"I think aging hair is great."

"Ouch," he says, a smile breaking his façade.

"No, this is a true story. I'm being dead honest when I say this," I offer. "I figured since you offered up Buffy, I could give you one of my most embarrassing nuggets."

His eyes dance with amusement. "Go on."

"I thought I was in love with Alex Trebek but it was just a teen crush."

"Seriously?"

I nod. "I used to watch *Jeopardy!* every night, and my mom had no idea why. I never cared about trivia, and I was an average student. It was that salt-and-pepper hair, man."

Oh my God, I just called my former boss hot in a round-about way. A man I hated like a half hour ago. I'm losing my edge.

"So, I'm just the hair to you. I see."

"You're more than the hair. It's your sparkling personality."

He laughs out loud, from deep in the recesses of his

throat. His laugh makes me giggle, one of those laughs that you can't help join in on.

"Rapid fire questions. You game?"

"Go for it. What else are we going to do?"

How about you take this dress off with your teeth—

"Favorite weekend activity?" I fire off.

"Brunch."

"Me too," I say, smacking him on the shoulder. "Bloody Mary or Mimosa?"

"Mimosa. Just leave the bottle," he says.

My cheeks warm. *I* love bottomless mimosas.

"Funniest thing to happen in the office since I've left?"

Smith looks to the ceiling for a thought. "Nessa messed up my birthday cake."

"You got a birthday cake? You've never wanted one before."

"This past year has been rough, okay?" He smiles wistfully, and I turn to a puddle. "She actually picked up the wrong one at the bakery. The cake was a huge eggplant emoji with a fondant Band-aid on it. It said, 'Congratulations on your vasectomy, Hank.'"

I cover my mouth at the image of this stoic, serious man receiving a penis cake.

"Did you eat it?"

"I did. I can't turn down cake. It was delicious."

I'm dying now, flopping over in laughter.

"The floor is disgusting, Cassie." I turn onto my back, convulsing in laughter. We catch eyes, and my giggles halt. His gaze shows that more than his stomach is hungry.

I sit up immediately, getting off my back. The less I remind either of us of sex, the better.

Now that Smith might not be *that* bad.

"Most embarrassing story?" Smith asks.

"I have many, but the most recent was when I fell off a Brew Bike," I answer with a laugh, remembering the fun Saturday activity I did with my friends. Until I broke skin.

He props his elbow on his knee and rests his chin on his hand. "Do tell."

"I'm a lightweight," I preface. "So, by the third brewery, I was *hammered*. My friends were peddling for me. I was wearing wedges, and my foot slipped and I stumbled off. I would've stayed on my feet, but my ankle twisted and I fell in a bush."

Smith is laughing now, a chortle deep and throaty.

Makes me want to get on my back again.

Smith's next question ups the ante.

"Are you dating anyone?"

Giddiness joined my nerves.

"Um...no, I'm not," I say.

"Why?" he asks.

He's not ready for this conversation. How men have disappointed me, one after another, and how I pledged to live alone forever. How celibacy is my new version of power and control.

How no one can live up to that shy and beautiful man Alex Trebek, may he rest in peace.

"I'm a lone wolf," I say. Then, I howl to make a point, but I feel like the biggest idiot. "I don't date."

"Interesting," he says. I let myself look at his face, turned away from me. I can't read his expression. Is he making small talk? Is he actually interested if I'm single or not?

I pause before I ask. "Why do you ask?"

"No reason," he says, his jaw tensing again.

"Okay," I say, looking down at my hands. "Do you know what time it is?"

Smith lifts his arm and readjusts his watch. "It's eight

o'clock. We have over an hour to go." His stomach rumbles again, and he looks down. "Wow, I'm sorry."

I have a granola bar in my purse, a snack I keep for emergencies. I fainted once when lunch was delayed so I always keep food on me. Hunger hasn't found me yet, since I ate a late lunch when I got wrapped up with editing a video this morning.

A granola bar is the least I can do for this man who is redeeming himself by the minute.

The wrapper rustles as I pull it out of my purse. "Here."

He looks down at it and then back up at me.

"Thank you," he says, holding out his hand. His hands are large and smooth so I pretend like it's a game of Operation and I *do not* brush my fingertips against him.

He rips open the green wrapper and breaks off a crumbling piece, dropping it in his mouth.

Smith breaks off piece after piece, offering me some in between his bites. I shake my head, and he happily continues.

"I haven't had one of these since college," he says.

"They're the best," I say. "Although they get *everywhere*."

"I think that's part of their charm," he says. He groans in satisfaction, and I bite my lip involuntarily. He rests his head back, his eyelids heavy with bliss.

My mind wanders to whether he looks like this after taking a woman to bed, after making love to Daniela, a woman so beautiful that he had to be stupid to let her go. How did it get so bad that someone cheated? What if it was him? That makes me stop whatever crush spiral I'm currently riding on.

"Thank you," he says, patting my knee. My breath catches. It's not sexual or inappropriate, but it tightens my chest and I exhale. There are those tingles again, my body responding to his touch.

"You're welcome," I say.

"Did you have a boyfriend when you worked for me?"

"Why do you assume it's a boyfriend?"

"Oh, I'm sorry," he says. "I didn't mean to assume..."

"It's okay. I'm unfortunately and dismally one hundred percent heterosexual," I say. "Creates a lot of problems for me."

"Why?" he asks. When he turns his head, our eyes catch, and there's my body being a thirsty hoe again. I honestly thought celibacy was making me stronger, but maybe I wasn't testing it properly.

Smith is *not* an option at all, even if I wasn't celibate.

"I did have a boyfriend. We broke up. Dating has been nothing but misery and I'm done chasing men. Three years ago, I tried singlehood on and haven't looked back. I've never been happier," I say, although I'm not sure it's true. I press my lips together and then offer, "Although, sometimes it gets lonely."

Expressing this is almost safe, to a man I will never see again.

Maybe this elevator is the only place I can be honest.

"I'm feeling the same way right now," he says, folding the wrapper between his fingers. "Daniela and I got divorced."

"Oh *no!*" I exclaim, pretending this was news to me and giving the best performance of my life. And I had my college boyfriend going for a full year that he was giving me orgasms from missionary.

"You knew, didn't you?" he asks.

"Nessa and Arlene told me," I admit.

Smith rubs his lips together again, his tongue slightly wetting them. For a brief moment, I thought what it would be like to touch my lips to his, but no. He sees me as a really good former employee. Nothing more.

"What else did they tell you?"

I tilt my head. "That someone cheated."

He nods again, his eyes anywhere but locked with mine. "Our divorce was finalized the week you quit."

That makes sense. How on edge he was, how his mind was probably somewhere else. I don't know why, but I scoot closer to him. Smith runs his fingers through his hair, and it's so sexy, I have to look away.

"I wanted it to be her so badly. The one. I wanted to be happy and have a family and live in Marin. Now, I don't know if that will happen."

Oh, Marin County. That beautiful and expensive suburb. I would love to live there too.

"I love San Francisco, but I don't see myself living here much longer. It's really noisy for ASMR purposes. You should see my apartment and the set-up I have. You would think a vampire lives there."

He smirks and I continue. "I really want space. Maybe some goats. I want to have children. I'll probably have to do it alone."

"Why alone?" When I turn to look at him, he stares at me, like I'm a mystery he's trying to solve.

He will find too much truth if he keeps searching so I turn away.

"I'm not sure I want to," I say. "Love doesn't last."

He says nothing, looking at his hands. I notice the stripe of white on his ring finger where his ring used to be.

"I have a hard time believing in love too," he says. "Especially lately."

"What happened? Between you and Daniela?" I ask.

He looks at his hands again. His silence tells me he has

no desire to talk about it, the way he swallows hard, his jaw clenches. My question won't be answered.

Am I feeling sympathy for him? Was I wrong?

"I have an easier question for you."

"Shoot."

"Do you still eat a Greek chicken salad every day?"

His face breaks into a grin. "Yes. Every day. I have to go get it myself now, though."

I used to get him one every day from the Mediterranean place around the corner from our office building. It became so consistent the owner had my order ready when I arrived. Smith barely looked up at me when I placed his lunch on his desk.

To get his attention, I started putting it onto the table in dramatic fashions. I once got a bunch of balloons to deliver it and...nothing. He never reacted; he just took the fork and opened the plastic bag without a word, without a thank you. When I first started, I wished him a happy lunch, but I stopped once I realized he treated me like I was invisible.

It doesn't matter that Smith is being nice to me now. He's only talking to me because he's stuck with me in an elevator and it's super boring.

This attraction I feel is because I haven't had sex in a really, really long time.

Smith fiddles with his cufflink.

The million-dollar question lingers between us, the bedazzled elephant in the room. He ignored me, he dismissed me. Now, he's acting like he likes me and his gaze is confusing the hell out of me.

I'll kick myself forever if I don't ask.

"Smith."

"Cassie." His gray-blue eyes grab mine, and I swallow.

Be brave.

"Why did you always ignore me? You never talked to me in the office."

Silence fills the elevator. Smith is struggling, looking everywhere but at me.

"It's complicated," he says.

"How so? I was always friendly toward you. I worked so hard for you. A 'thank you,' a 'good job' goes a long way with me. I messed up *once*. In five years. That was it."

"You didn't mess up," he says. "I have a hard time admitting I'm wrong. Just ask my ex-wife."

He looks at me with an impenetrable gaze. Is there hunger there? Does he want to kiss me?

Do I want him to?

"I wanted to talk to you tonight to say I'm sorry," Smith says. "I take full responsibility for the mistake with that case."

I didn't know I needed to hear that until the words left his lips. Those perfect lips.

His swallow is audible as he looks down and then back up.

I don't think about the consequences. All I want is for him to touch me.

He rubs his palms together. "I've missed you every day since you quit."

What? I laugh nervously. "Because I did such a good job?"

He pauses, and my body goes rigid. I brace for the impact of his words, but when they come, they still jolt me.

"More than that."

4

A ghast. I am aghast.

"That makes no sense," I blurt out.

His stare bores into me. "I know."

"You *missed* me."

"I did," he says. "Very much."

The way he says it is more than "I miss your salad delivery."

Right?

"Missed me how?" I regret asking the nanosecond I say it.

"I could trust you. I don't trust many people in my life."

I relax, but also my stomach churns. Okay, it wasn't a romantic "I miss you," just "I could trust you to do your job. I could depend on you."

It's totally different. And totally devastating for some reason.

"I was a dick to you," Smith says. "I was under an incredible amount of pressure. My personal life was disintegrating, and I took you for granted. I'm so sorry for yelling at you."

"Apology accepted," I say, trying to keep the tears at bay.

I swallow them down. I'm not sure why I'm getting so emotional that I got the apology I was craving and the vindication that feels anything but satisfying.

Feelings swirl within me, confusing me, and I stand up to avoid being close to him. This is why I don't put myself in situations where I get close to men. There's too much risk for me since every relationship I've attempted has failed at a hundred percent.

My heart cannot take another pummel so it's best to get out of this elevator as soon as possible.

"I'm going to ask for an update." I hit the bell button again.

The intercom crackles on. "Uh, hello?"

"Yes, I wanted to get an update on the technician?"

"Still an hour and a half. Maybe two."

I check my watch. "We've already been in here for an hour."

"I'm sorry."

Another apology I'm not excited about.

The intercom quiets, and the silence in this elevator is so loud.

My pacing begins again, my arms tightly wrapped around myself.

"Are you going to sit down again or..." he asks.

"I'll stand, thank you," I say. I move from one side to the other, three steps and three steps the other way.

I have to ask it. If he thought I was such a good employee, that he could *trust* me, why did he treat me like I was invisible?

"I have one question." I hold up a finger for emphasis. "Why did you ignore me the *entire* time I worked there? If I was such a valuable asset and you trusted me, why didn't you tell me that?"

Smith looks at the ground, reaching for his cufflink again. "Like I said, it's complicated."

I sit down, draping my skirt over my knees as I stretch my legs out. "What's complicated?"

He says nothing and then I ask differently. "What happened?"

I expect him to retreat, to deflect. Instead, he speaks instantly.

"I had a lot of things going on in my personal life. My ex-wife and I didn't fit quite right, and honestly, we never did. But the final nail on the coffin was that she had an affair with someone else," he says, his lips pursing with the confession. "I thought she would be the mother of my children, and now she's nothing. We're not even friends."

That is a lot more information than I was expecting. His anguished face makes him look vulnerable, like those sad dogs I feel sorry for and then cry at in the animal shelter commercials.

I pat his folded hands. The touch sizzles, but I rest my hand there anyway, since I apparently haven't learned anything. A mature man flashes his baby blues at me, and I'm Jell-O.

"You could've talked to me," I say, pressing my hand to my chest. "And your divorce still doesn't explain why after *five years* of working together, you never talked to me. Why you never told me how much you trusted me or depended on me. It would've made my working experience *a lot* better, and I wouldn't have had to quit and you wouldn't have to miss such a stellar employee."

"I told you, it was more than that," Smith says, turning back toward me. His pupils are fire, staring me down. His lips press into each other and I don't know what to do. What this is.

"I don't know what you mean," I say.

"I'm just going to say it," he says. He pauses and lets out a huff of quaking breath. "I was ridiculously, irrationally, insanely attracted to you."

My mouth drops for the seventh time tonight.

I've been called cute. I've been called pretty. But there's no way a man who's had a woman like Daniela could be attracted to me. Her hair is black silk, a freaking hair commercial success story. Her skin barely has a blemish while I have a volcano brewing on my chin under a layer of makeup.

Daniela always seemed like a poised, classy woman while I'm the opposite. I take up space. A man or two has called me "mouthy."

Me being me, I need answers.

"Was?" I ask.

"Still am," Smith says. He flips my hand over and drags his fingertips along my turned-up palm.

I bite my lip. It feels so amazing to be touched by someone other than myself. My parents hug me and my friends hug me, but I forget how the touch of a man is different, more sensual.

Especially a man who is ridiculously, irrationally, insanely attracted to me.

"Why?"

"You're intelligent, kind. I saw you around the office, caring about everyone. You have so much fun and are so... joyful. I knew I needed to keep my distance. I shoved my attraction down so far and pretended like you didn't exist. If I did that, maybe I could save my marriage. I knew if I got close to you, I would be a bigger fucking asshole than I already was."

He drags his fingers along my forearm and my eyelashes flutter closed.

"Do you think I'm an asshole?" Smith asks.

"No, I don't think you're an asshole," I whisper, turning my head. My breath is heavy and loud. A tiny moan escapes my lips.

"Cassie," he says. I can feel his breath mingle with mine. "I..."

I grab his shirt and pull him to me. His lips slam into mine. I taste the sweetness of the granola bar I gave him and smell the spice of his cologne. His lips are soft, just like I knew they would be. His fingers touch the base of my skull, lace through my hair.

Everything is firing.

My face grows hot with this kiss, his tongue dipping in to find mine. It's passion, a simmer that explodes. My stomach churns with the rabid butterflies, my skin singing with his touch.

I'm making out with my former boss, and damn, it feels good.

He pulls me onto his lap so I'm facing him. My legs wrap around him as he runs his fingers down my spine, hot streaks of pleasure where his touch burns me. I buck against his hard cock straining against his pants, my sex molding to his as we devour each other.

The world moves around us in this tiny elevator, our connection drowning out the noise of the machine.

Everything falls away, and all that matters is Smith's hands on me, his lips on my neck, his hand lifting my hair.

I don't notice the elevator doors opening behind me. With one strap of my dress off my shoulder, straddling my ex-boss.

"Called it," Vincent, one of the grooms, says from behind me.

I turn slowly, like a heroine in a horror movie. I turn to see Vincent, my best friend and man of the hour, standing in the middle of a sea of his wedding guests, all who witnessed me sucking the face of the man I hated an hour and a half ago.

5

———

"It's not what it looks like," I say, dismounting from Smith's lap. My legs wobble when I stand up, and Smith stands as well, wiping something on his black dress pants.

"You have to cover me," Smith whispers. I shiver from his breath on my ear. "I have an issue."

I look back quickly and stifle a laugh. Pretty proud of myself since Smith has a raging, *noticeable* hard-on.

Smith follows me closely out of the elevator, and we pass a man in a gray jumpsuit and a ballcap with the hotel's logo on it.

"Thank you for getting us out," I say politely to the technician.

"You're welcome. It doesn't look like it was too bad in there. You probably wish it was longer," he says with a wink. Once he registers my grave expression, his smile disappears. "I'm sorry I said that. Please don't get me fired..."

"I won't. You're kinda right," I say, smirking.

Smith is standing so close to me to calm himself down. Meanwhile, I am anything but calm.

"Do you have to stand so close to me?" I say under my breath.

"I'm almost fine. Please be my shield," he says.

I hear all sorts of voices as we pass. Smith ducks into the bathroom, but the whispers do not stop.

Were they kissing?

Didn't she quit?

Is anyone going to tell Daniela?

I knew *there was something going on with them.*

I can't believe I kissed him.

I can't believe it was that amazing.

My hair in my face annoys me, so I pull out my emergency hair tie and my phone.

I don't care it if it's a wedding and I just got a blowout. I do my best thinking with my hair in a messy bun.

My hands tremble as I re-buckle my shoes, and my legs are still unsure as I stand up on them.

Usually Vincent would be sliding up a chair to get all the details, but the DJ has cleared the dance floor for him and his love. I will probably get lots of text messages at two a.m.

"Mr. and Mr. Ricci-Jones are about to start their first dance, so gather around them to feel their love," he announces.

Quentin, Smith's best friend and fellow partner, looks dapper in his navy blue plaid suit as he offers a hand to his groom. Vincent's baby blue plaid suit compliments his new husband's as they embrace and sway to Etta James's "At Last."

I watch Quentin's mother and aunts, draped in gold and navy, swaying as they watch him happy, at last. I watch Quentin's father standing next to Vincent's father, clinging to each other, both so proud and happy. Vincent's mom has passed, but I know she's looking down at him, proud of his baby boy.

Quentin looks at my best friend like he hung the world, and I feel an ache in my gut.

I realized long ago that romantic love might never happen for me.

I've been disappointed too many times. With a long-term relationship that failed, with all those dates that never went anywhere. With short relationships that fizzled and ended for so many different reasons. How I begged men to love me and they called me crazy.

As the song builds to a crescendo of violins and emotions, I see Smith walking out of the bathroom, buttoning his jacket.

Our eyes catch, and his mouth flicks to a smirk, disarming me. The memory of his lips on me send pulses of heat through my core.

I can think of a million reasons it won't work with him.

Nessa appears in front of me, cutting off Smith's prowl. He turns around quickly in such a dorky, cute way, I can't help but grin.

"Spill. How was it?"

The best kiss I've ever had. My chin still stings with his scruff burn, but if I close my eyes, I can still feel his fingers on my face.

I could orgasm at least every day for a week replaying that over and over.

My hopes are reaching new heights, and it's best I just cut it off at the knees now.

All I see with Smith is a big, future broken heart.

"I need to get out of here," I say. Nessa's black eyebrows knit together in confusion.

"Why do you want to leave? Vincent says they're going to play 'Total Eclipse of the Heart' soon. For you."

That *is* my jam. I bite my lip.

"Also, the cake. White cake with lemon filling. Vincent promised me that was one of the options. Our favorite."

God, I love that too.

"I just...um..."

I'm so scared. Smith is the epitome of everything that has hurt me in a man, in an irresistible, virile man package.

The only way to stay happy is if this never happens between us.

"Oh my God, he's coming," I say as I dunk behind her and under the table.

"Why are you acting like you shoplifted?" Nessa asks. "It looked pretty hot in the elevator."

It was. It really, really was.

"Cassie," Smith says, and I say *dammit* under my breath. I stand from my crouching position behind my friend.

"Why are you hiding?" he asks.

"I dropped...my eyelash." I pinch my left eyelash set and smile. "All better."

"I'm glad we got out," Smith says. He looks down and then back up again.

"So am I," I agree with a fake laugh and a dismissive hand flip.

Please leave. You look way too good, and I want to eat your face again.

"I have to go," I blurt out, and I immediately flip open the Uber app. At this moment, I regret getting rid of my car. Right after I quit the firm, I sold it to save on expenses. I now rely on public transport and Ubers, and it's never been a problem. Until now.

"I have my car. I can take you home," Smith offers.

"No!" I yell. I'll straddle him again in his driver's seat in some parking garage, I just know it.

I wander over to the gifts and guest book table, scribbling my well wishes on the guest book picture frame and dropping off my card in a flower-adorned wicker basket. Smith, unfortunately, follows me.

"Total Eclipse of the Heart" begins playing. I *will not* turn around, Bonnie Tyler.

"The wedding isn't over," he says matter-of-factly.

"I know. But I have to go."

"That kiss was really, really nice," he whispers, leaning in as we walk at a mall-walker pace toward the stairs. I'm not getting in an elevator right now, possibly not ever again. "More than nice."

His voice burns my skin like hot metal, and I need to remind myself to breathe.

I reach the stairs. Now I'm in an impossible situation. Stairwells have always creeped me out, since the lighting always casts low-budget horror movie feels and who knows who is lurking, waiting to snatch me. The only way I'm getting out of a kidnapping is talking, and I'm too exhausted to talk right now.

My need for security trumps my desire to avoid Smith so I don't tell him to get lost.

We are quiet for two flights of stairs.

He's the first one to speak. "I would like to see you again. After the wedding. Preferably not in an elevator."

"I don't think that's a good idea."

The stairwell echoes with my heels as I try not to hold the decrepit handrail, probably lined with hepatitis. He follows me at four steps behind.

"I'm not following you. I'm just making sure you get into the car safely."

When we reach the ground floor, I breathe a sigh of relief to feel the warmth of the lobby, with its gold details and high ceilings, and tourists milling in and out. There is a family at the entrance, standing there to absorb the splendor.

I turn around, facing Smith. His hands are in his pockets again. His salt-and-pepper hair a mess, probably from my hands.

I outstretch my hand to shake so there is no confusion. "It was a pleasure to see you again. I forgive you."

"You forgive me?" he asks with a smirk. That devilish tweak of his mouth could liquefy me into goo, but Uber saves. My phone vibrates that my car is approaching.

"My car is here. Gotta go, bye," I say, running past the family. I practically dive into a Nissan Altima.

"Are you Carlos?" I ask, remembering the girl who ran into the wrong car and then was taken somewhere and murdered.

"Yes. Are you Cassie?" he asks. I nod and look back. Smith is standing outside, the light of the hotel illuminating him, making him a shadow.

A new cocktail of relief and sadness fill my chest as we drive further away from the Octavo.

"Are you having a good night, Cassie?"

I still look back although I lost sight of Smith three blocks ago. "I got stuck in the elevator for an hour."

"Oh my God, that's crazy. I hate small spaces. That would be my nightmare."

"It wasn't so bad."

My fingertips go to my lips, where Smith's lips were just a few minutes before. They are still warm to the touch, and my body still remembers what it felt like.

His hands on my waist. His fingers in my hair. His lips so close to my breast so I'm now breathing hard in this Uber.

"Are you okay? I can turn on the air," Carlos offers.

"I'm fine, thank you."

Except the inside of me is screaming.

If I decide to get back out there in the dating world, Smith is not the man I should choose. He is twelve years older than me, broken, cheated on. Newly divorced. Lonely. Nothing worse than a brooding, sensitive, great kisser when I've had a long, storied history with that type and had sworn them off until about ten minutes ago.

I need our group chat. My best friend, Erin, myself, our married friend Sarah, and Raegan, our newest friend.

Me: I need brunch tomorrow ASAP.

Erin: I love brunch. Done.

Sarah: Let me see if Jin has anything going on. What time?

Raegan: I'm in!!!!!! 10?

Me: That sounds great. How about Home Plate?

Erin: YES. Bottomless mimosas. ALL THE YES.

Raegan: Can't wait.

My friends will help me figure this out.

For now, I have a date with a British baking show, a bottle of white wine, and my strongest lip mask to remove the memory of Smith's lips from mine.

"I CANNOT BELIEVE YOU, CASS," Erin says, tilting back her mimosa. "I can*not*."

We sit under the big chalk menu as we pound mimosas. I usually choose health, but today is all about the baked goods. All the scones and pancakes.

My friends represent the sliding scale of relationship status. Sarah has been shackled up for years, marrying her high school sweetheart at twenty-three and immediately popping out one kid and then another a few years later. Erin recently started dating Landon, an app tycoon whom she met on an airplane. Raegan is a relatively new friend who fits in easily with my OG crew; I met her when we bonded over a rather awkward yin yoga class where the lady in front of us broke wind very very loudly...and then proceeded to give a five-minute apology in the middle of downward dog, blaming it on prunes.

I just told them everything. The run-in, the elevator, the kiss.

"What does Smith look like?" Sarah asks, typing into her phone and barely looking up. Her husband Jin is alone with the kids and cannot find their daughter Emma's favorite toy, a stuffed rabbit, and supposedly she is losing her mind. The way Sarah's phone is going off, Jin's losing his mind as well.

I pull up a photo from the firm's website and show it around the table.

"Holy shit, Cassie, he is hot!" Raegan says. "Was he not a good kisser?"

"He was excellent," I say.

"And he didn't ask you out or get your number or anything?"

I would like to see you again. After the wedding. Preferably not in an elevator. I shake my head.

Erin looks at the photo and leans back. "Wasn't he married?"

I shake my head. "They got divorced. She cheated on him."

"I cannot believe you. You kiss possibly the hottest man I've ever seen and don't follow up for a phone number, a handle, *nothing*," Erin says, popping the raspberry garnish into her mouth. "Is he actually terrible?"

I cross my arms. "No, he's..."

Dorky. Thoughtful. Sexy.

Screams "pain, heartache, and bad decisions."

"Oh no, I know that look," Erin says, pointing a finger at me.

"What look?" Raegan asks.

Sarah doesn't look up from her phone. "Here we go again."

Raegan looks confused.

One of the most refreshing things about Raegan is she's only known me single. She doesn't know how needy I can be, how insane I felt when I was barely treading water in the dating pool.

How my friends saw the red flags of every man I dated and I ignored each one. How I fall hard and get hurt even harder.

Nothing like a huge dick against my lady parts to awaken the dumb bitch within me.

Sarah drops her phone in her purse and opens her hands. "Okay, I think Jin found Emma's rabbit, so we're good. Now, single people problems."

"Why not pursue Smith then?" Raegan asks.

"Don't encourage her," Erin says, pointing with a finger. "Trust me."

"I'm better now," I say. "I've had three years in my single detox. Maybe it's not Smith, but maybe I should get back out there again."

Erin and Sarah give each other a look.

A flash of me on Smith's lap, kissing him until my lips hurt, is summoned like a demon from the Hellmouth on *Buffy*.

Raegan claps her hands together. "Perfect! You can come with me to a singles' event next weekend. It's on a boat."

"I don't know..." I literally just started considering

throwing my hat back in the San Francisco dating scene.

"Oh, come on," Raegan says. "My friend from work bailed, and I have this extra ticket. I *can't* go alone. It will be *so* fun. It's all-you-can-drink, and I'm pretty sure there will be crab cakes."

I pause. I love me a good crab cake.

"Please?" Raegan asks. "You're my only other single friend. You can be my wing woman."

Raegan has been a great friend ever since Erin started dating Landon and spent most nights of the week with him. She has also been an incredible sport, letting me brush her hair for ASMR videos. Raegan frequently dyes her hair fun colors, so I've used her on my channel liberally.

Her green eyes plead with me. "Fine. I'll go."

"Yay!" she cheers.

We order, and they make fun of me for how I dismissed Smith for the rest of the brunch.

I am firm in my decision. Smith is not the one. Definitely not the *first* one to get me back out there.

Still, I remember the way his eyes lit up when he talked about *Buffy the Vampire Slayer*, how he looked so hurt as he talked about how his marriage fell apart.

The way his fingertips felt on my neck as we kissed.

That kiss didn't mean anything. We were simply stuck together in an elevator, in peril, after a lengthy, in-depth conversation that mimicked intimacy and feelings.

As I sip my mimosa, as my friends complain about their significant others and Raegan details yet another date where she disqualified a guy for a silly reason, I wonder if Smith is just as messed up from our time in the elevator as I am.

6

"This is promising," Raegan says as she steps onto the huge boat hosting the singles mixer. The night is chilly, the sky an inky blue, and the sparkle of downtown glows in the distance. The boat sways gently, docked at the marina so singletons can hop on, hoping to find the love of their life. It's bright and full of promise, but I have one mission only.

I'm going to find my friend some dick.

Not me. Kissing Smith freaked me out so much that I'm safe back in my single-lady cocoon, warm and content.

I'm down to thinking about Smith maybe five times a day. It's been four days since I looked at his picture on the firm's website.

I feel like I'm cured.

"Do you see anyone interesting?" she asks. I look around. No good prospects for Raegan yet. And definitely not for me.

"I need a drink," I proclaim, and Raegan follows me into the galley, up to the bartender clad in a white shirt and black vest.

"One gin and tonic," I say.

Instead of Raegan giving her drink order, I hear a man's voice, running my blood chunks-of-iceberg cold.

"Make it two," he says.

When I turn around, I grab my chest.

Smith Cooper Kennedy, looking way too good, standing right in front of me.

"Who is this, Cassie?" Raegan says, stabbing me in the side with her sharp elbow.

"Raegan, this is my old boss Smith Kennedy. Mr. Kennedy, this is my friend, Raegan."

"You're back to calling me Mr. Kennedy. Interesting."

I swallow the hard lump in my throat. Smith looks sexier than ever, wearing a fitted gray shirt with his sleeves rolled to his elbows and a pair of black pants fitting him *too* well.

I can see the outline of the impressive bulge I've felt, and I have to look away.

My body used to tense with disdain, but now it's tensing for another reason. I want to jump him and eat his face.

Raegan leans in. "Oh, is this the one? You know, the elevator?"

I want this boat to sink right now because yes, Raegan, this is the man I'm trying to forget.

"Yes," I say through clenched teeth.

"It's a pleasure to meet you," Raegan says, shaking his hand. "Are you also looking for a special someone?"

His eyes drill into me. "Just one."

I slap my hand on the counter of the bar to steady myself. Did he get more good-looking? I want to pull him into a closet or a bathroom and have my way with him. Then I remind myself why I'm here: Raegan needs a wing woman. That's my only mission tonight.

"Just one," Raegan repeats. "Is that, by chance, Cassie?"

"Shut up, Raegan," I seethe.

"Maybe," Smith says, tucking a twenty in the tip jar.

He's a good tipper too? Consider my panties officially wet.

The bartender sets down two gin and tonics and a Moscow Mule for Raegan. I sip the drink immediately, hoping the gin can knock some sense into me.

Smith is not a viable option.

Broken.

Recently divorced.

Might still be an asshole.

Dick might be too big for me.

I wince. The last one is not a good excuse.

"Well, we better go and mingle. I would hate for women to think you're interested in us," I say, pulling an unwilling Raegan away.

"What if I am?"

"Have a wonderful night!" I say, pulling a protesting Raegan away from that conversation.

"He's even better-looking than his photo," Raegan says, looking behind her. "Are you out of your mind, Cassie?"

"I am not. I am level-headed. I cannot start something with that man."

"Why not?" Raegan asks loudly. I slap my hand over her mouth.

"Like I said, I'm only here for moral support. I want to find *you* a boyfriend."

"You were game at brunch last weekend, and now you're running away from *that*?" Raegan says. "He's the kind of good-looking that you know he has a shit ton of money. Like a *shit ton*."

I roll my eyes. "I don't need to marry a devastatingly

handsome and successful man who wears a watch that costs more than my rent to be happy and complete and whole."

Raegan's green eyes narrow on me. "Who said anything about getting married? I was talking about sex. Accepting lavish gifts. Being a *sugar baby*."

No," I yell, and people look at me. I lean in. "It's just not my journey."

"He's still looking at you." Raegan's sharp elbow hits me again, and we look across the deck. Smith slowly sips his gin and tonic from the side, not through the straw. The way his lips cover the side of the glass throws a vision into my head of him. Between my legs, covering my clit with those perfect lips. Sucking, licking...

"Did you just moan?" Raegan asks.

"No," I say, turning so I can rest my forearms on the railing and avoid his penetrating gaze.

"You should talk to him. He hasn't stopped looking at you," Raegan says.

After I get my breath under control, I turn back to her with a smile. "Okay, so who here is your type? What about that guy?"

I covertly point to a good-looking guy in glasses and a patterned shirt.

She scrunches her button nose. "Too nerdy."

"That's not nerdy. You know what Smith told me in the elevator?" I say with a laugh. "He's into *Buffy the Vampire Slayer*. So nerdy, right?"

"Right," Raegan agrees, eyes narrowing further. "I think you need to talk to Smith."

"About what? There's no reason for me to talk to him."

Raegan now folds her arms against her chest and flicks an eyebrow. "Didn't you kiss him?"

"So?" I say.

"You don't kiss random people. You haven't kissed anyone the whole time I've known you."

Smith's eyes still glaze over my skin, causing shivers. No, that's just San Francisco.

"Think about it. I need to do a lap. I heard somewhere that women are easier to approach if they're alone," Raegan says. She takes me in a warm hug and kisses my cheek. "Just talk to him."

"Maybe," I say as Raegan leaves me all alone on the deck.

The minute she walks away, the men notice and hone in.

The first brave man approaches, and I tilt up my chin. Turning down men can be fun.

"Your dress is really pretty," the man says.

I look down at my navy blue maxi-dress and back up. "Thanks."

"You know where it would look even better?" he asks. I close my eyes to brace for the blow. "My floor."

"Okay, enough," Smith says, sandwiching himself between the pickup artist and myself.

"Hey man, I was just getting started."

"You need a lot more than that for this caliber of woman," he says.

The pickup artist points to Smith. "Are you okay with this?"

Smith being so close to me, his pheromones making me powerless?

"Absolutely," I say.

"We have business to attend to," he says, offering my arm like we're going to a ball. I take it, and he leads me into the warm air of the cabin.

We find a gender-neutral bathroom, and he pulls me in.

Another enclosed space. I should escape.

Instead, I cock out my leg from the slit on my dress like I'm Angelina Jolie.

He locks the door, and I cross my arms across the cleavage I've got, which isn't much.

Smith turns around, his breath oddly rough.

"You changed your phone number," he says.

I lift an eyebrow in surprise. "I got a new phone six months ago."

Smith places his hands on his hips again, turning around to face the door. Since I'm a weak woman, I check out his ass.

"How did you know I would be here?" I ask.

"Vincent," Smith says. I'm not sure whether to call Vincent and yell at him or Venmo him twenty bucks.

Smith pivots, and I almost melt. His salt-and-pepper hair is perfectly styled, and his eyes crinkle at the sides. His shirt is doing some work since his muscles are straining against the fabric.

I hop on the sink, the countertop barely large enough for my butt. I'm wearing a dress, so I cross my legs, but they could open at any moment.

"I can't stop thinking about you," he says, looking at the ground. "I thought I was fine and then I saw you again at the wedding and all the feelings I've bottled up came rushing back. That kiss made it worse. You said men don't chase you, but I *will*. If you want."

I expect him to rush me, take my lips with his. My lips are parted; I'm waiting. He still stands there.

"That kiss was pretty great," I say. I lean forward, letting my neckline gape. I'm not wearing a bra.

He runs his tongue across his lips, and I almost gasp.

Why am I like this?

I spent the last week actively avoiding any obsession

over Smith, and now, I'm giving in after two sips of an alco-
holic beverage.

I uncross my legs, and I lean back onto my palms.

I hope he doesn't make me beg.

"What are you doing?" Smith asks, his eyes fixed on me.

"Nothing," I say. "Just getting comfortable."

"I'm not going to do anything until you say so."

"I thought you were an alpha," I say, my legs parting
more. Smith hasn't touched me yet, but if he doesn't soon, I
will.

"I am," he says, stepping closer. "I'm also a man with
values and scruples."

"I want your scruples all over me," I say, then wince
because that makes no goddamn sense.

He laughs, and I crook my finger. Smith crosses the
room in one step. His mouth covers mine, and it's the kiss in
the elevator times one thousand.

He kisses me like he's starved, nibbling on my lip,
sweeping his tongue against mine in a torrid dance. My
hands go through his hair as he presses his hand into my
lower back, fingertips inches from my ass. Smith pulls me
closer, his hard length pressing against me, and my hips
buck involuntarily, like our bodies recognize each other's.

I can't breathe, but I can't come up for air. A tiny moan
leaves my mouth, which would usually embarrass me, but I
don't care. All that matters is his hands on me, his cock
against my clit, his mouth on me.

His touch is hesitant, but I want no doubt in his mind. I
dip my hand between us, feeling him through his pants.
He groans, low and guttural, hips bucking against my
palm.

Holy shit, he is long and thick, growing stronger in my
hand.

I grab his hand and place it on my breast. His thumb plays with my nipple.

I pull down his zipper, but he wiggles away.

His eyes lock with mine. "You first."

Biting my lip, I watch Smith trail down my body, licking the top of my breast, pulling aside my dress strap to take a nipple in his mouth. My head rolls back, slamming against the mirror.

I might have a concussion, but I don't care.

I gather my dress hem, and he pushes my legs wider. I'm panting, I'm so turned on and ready. He says nothing but drapes one of my legs over his shoulder and leans in.

In my experience, men removed the underwear as soon as possible, but Smith takes his time. He kisses the fabric where my clit is and she responds. A first spark of flame swirls within my core, and my eyes flutter closed.

His finger dips in, and I hope he feels how slick my walls are, how ready I am for him as he continues to suck my clit through the underwear.

"God, yes," I whisper. His mouth knows just what to do. I buck against his mouth, silently begging him to pull my underwear to the side, pull them off, rip through them.

Just get them off me.

"Stop teasing," I say.

"What?" he looks up, pulling his fingers out of me and licking them. "Do you want me to taste you for real?"

"Yes," I say.

He says nothing but leans down again. He hooks his thumbs and pulls the underwear down my legs, excruciatingly slowly. I shake my legs to kick the underwear away, and his kisses on my inner thighs makes my body pulse.

When he licks my bare clit, I arch my back and moan, louder and more primal.

"Fuck yes," I scream as he bobs his head like the professional clit jockey he is. His tongue laps and swirls and sucks and drives me to the brink of being a mad woman.

It's been so long since I've had a tongue on me, much less a tongue that knows what it's doing. It's not long until I come undone, the payoff long and violent, my body vibrating as he continues to indulge. When my orgasm settles, he kisses my thigh and flips my dress to cover me.

His cock is in my hand when there's a loud knock at the door. We freeze, his lips covered with my arousal.

"Madam and whoever is in there with Madam. This is Barbara, the owner of Love of Your Life Bay Cruises. We were alerted that there were some loud sounds coming from this bathroom of a sexual nature. Please make yourself decent and exit the bathroom immediately."

7

I believe no woman should be embarrassed for receiving or giving pleasure.

However.

Try getting caught receiving oral sex from your former boss in a boat bathroom, when you've vowed to stay single forever. Mortification does not even begin to describe what I'm feeling right now.

Smith offers a hand, and I take it to jump off of the counter.

"Come out now," Barbara demands from the other side of the door.

"One moment," I yell.

Smith's face is bright red, and mine doesn't look much better.

He takes his time, splashing water on his face. I arrange my skirt so it falls evenly and I double-check my ass in the mirror. Smith smacks it, and I give him a flirty glare.

"Did I just hear spanking?!"

"Oh, get your panties out of a twist, Barbara," I say, and

Smith laughs, covering his mouth. His arm looped around my middle makes me all gooey like caramel.

"You have to cover me again," Smith says. I look down, and I grin. He has a hard-on, just like last time.

Aw, memories.

He presses his body against my backside, kissing my neck before we open the door. His arms around my waist, his body glued to me, we walk out like our ankles are tied together. I don't know how pressing his cock into my ass crack will settle him down, but I'm not complaining.

A small crowd of people have gathered, with a severe-looking woman with a lip snarl and crossed arms at the center. That has to be Barbara, missing her calling as a harsh headmistress in a movie with a spunky child protagonist.

There are other people, including a janitor whose inner dialogue I want to hear so bad and a few women either proud of me or disgusted I snatched up such a good-looking man.

"Barbara," Smith says with a respectful nod.

"Babs," I say.

"This is a wholesome singles event, and you two...you two..." she reprimands, clearly not able to find the words. An exasperated huff comes out from her red lipstick, slightly smudged around the outline.

I truly wonder when the last time she got laid was.

"We apologize if we've made any guests uncomfortable," Smith says. "I'm just crazy about her."

He squeezes me to him, and electric currents flow through me. I never believed people when they claimed sparks when they touched their lover, but I am proven wrong. Everything I know for sure is shifting.

Maybe I didn't know anything at all.

"Come with me," Barbara says.

Smith pulls away from me, and we follow Barbara into the belly of the boat, down carpeted stairs to a non-descript white door. Barbara motions for us to go inside. We find a tiny office with two chairs for visitors. We sit down, careful not to touch each other.

Barbara sits down slowly in her chair. "We can't go back to the dock until the event is over, but you two *must* separate."

"I'll stay here," Smith offers. "She came with a friend, and I've gotten what I came here for tonight."

Remembering that beautiful head of hair between my legs, I blush. Hard.

Barbara's eyes flick between the two of us. She looks at me like I'm the biggest harlot to ever step foot on this boat. "You won't find another man? Or woman?"

"She better not," Smith says.

I didn't know it was possible to blush even harder, but I do. Usually, I would be disgusted at such a show of alpha possessiveness, but it's intoxicating coming from Smith.

"Okay," Barbara says, her shoulders and face relaxing. "Sir, you will stay here, and miss, you can go up to the deck. No more funny business."

"I promise," I say. Before I leave, I drop my head down and steal a kiss from Smith.

Now, *he's* blushing.

"Wait for me!" I yell dramatically to him as I leave the office.

I walk back up the stairs on shaky legs, the heat still present between them. I mill through the crowd, looking for my friend.

I pick out Raegan's purple hair immediately. She's talking to a man who wears desperation as a cologne.

"Hi!" Raegan says. She pulls away from the man, her smile disappearing once we are away from him. "Thank goodness. His breath smelled."

We walk away, and I fluff my hair since I don't know what to do with my hands.

"What happened?" Raegan whispers. "You look different."

"Well..." I begin, putting my hands on my hips. I cannot contain my smile. and Raegan's eyes go as big as quarters.

"Did you have sex? On a boat?"

"Yes, but no penetration," I say with a finger point. Leaning in, I whisper, "Smith went down on me in the bathroom."

"Up top," Raegan says, holding up a hand for a high-five. I smack it, and then we both shake our hands out since it was an enthusiastic (and hard) high five.

"We got caught, so Smith is in timeout in Barbara's office."

"Who's Barbara?"

I point to Barbara, who is watching me like a rookie FBI agent.

"Oh," Raegan says. "She looks scary."

"She is," I say. "I have to kill time before Smith's sprung from boat jail."

"Let's just have some fun. The two of us," Raegan says.

"Sounds good to me," I say. "I need another drink."

"Me too."

Raegan speaks fluent French, so she spends the rest of the evening pretending like she doesn't speak English when a guy approaches us. We find the bow of the boat and do our own *Titanic* reenactment. When they start playing music, we do interpretive dances, and most of the men stare at us. Some are intrigued, and I do not trust them for that since our dancing was *awful.*

When the boat docks, I feel giddiness in my soul.

Without a doubt, I'm going to get laid tonight.

"YOU'RE FREE!" I say with outstretched arms, waiting on the dock. Smith smiles shyly as he joins me on dry land. He picks me up and spins me around.

"I learned a lot in my time behind bars," he says. "Most of all, that I want to spend the rest of the evening with you."

"I feel the same way," I say.

"What do you want to do?"

"Go back to your place."

Smith looks down and then back up at me with a devilish grin. "Sure."

We have to wait for an Uber since the event just finished, but we get in one eventually. It's a quiet ride, except for the rap music the driver plays, but Smith grabs my hand and holds it like we're dating.

It scares me and thrills me, all at once.

When we arrive at his building, we step out, and the wind from the bay chills me to a shiver. He wraps his arm around me, pulling me to close to him for warmth. He buzzes himself in, and we walk across a carpeted lobby to the elevator bank.

"I'm triggered," I say, and he lets out a hearty laugh.

"When the elevator situation happened, I talked to my landlord about this, and they're serviced way more frequently than the ones at the Octavo."

"Still nervous," I say when the doors open.

I walk in first, and he follows me. As soon as the doors

close, his lips are on mine, his hands cradling my face, his thumbs playing with my earrings. It's a kiss that turns my knees to pudding, makes me question every truth I know about myself.

"One kiss in an elevator wasn't enough," Smith says. "Plus, this makes me forget that I'm terrified of being stuck again."

"It distracted me too," I say.

When it dings for his floor, the tenth, I breathe out a sigh of relief that we made it and follow him down the hall to his apartment. He pushes the key into the lock, looking back at me as he opens. When he flips on the switch, I gasp.

It's the most beautiful apartment I've ever been in.

Clean white and neutral grays—simple, elegant. Large picture windows encompass the space, and the shine of the city overwhelms me.

This apartment is complete opposite to my tiny four hundred square foot apartment with clothes and video props and video equipment strewn about and one tiny window.

"Wine?" Smith asks, and I nod. He walks to his kitchen as I walk past his taupe couches to a side table with a vase holding white flowers and a single silver frame. I hunch down to get a better look.

It's a younger Smith, with dark ink hair in a graduation gown, flanked by two older people. He holds a smile wider than I've ever seen on his face.

"Your parents?" I ask.

"Yes," Smith says, handing me a glass of wine. I take a sip and let the flavor roll over my tongue. Smith's eyes stay on me as he sips his own wine. "That's my law school graduation."

"Are you close to them?"

"Very close," Smith says. "They live in San Rafael. It's where I want to settle eventually. When I meet the right woman and start a family."

That comment roasts my insides. The way he looks at me makes me think I'm on the short list for Smith's future baby momma.

No, he can't be thinking that. A couple standalone kisses and an amazing orgasm don't mean we'll fall in love or even date. My future of adopting multiple foster children and having a farm with chickens and sassy goats is still possible.

This feels too perfect. The wheels are bound to fall off.

I know this, but I still keep driving.

"Do you like music?" he asks, walking toward me, resting a hand on my waist.

"Sure," I say.

"Alexa, play my relaxing playlist on shuffle."

A slow, seductive jazz starts, throwing a gauzy haze over this night.

"Jazz, huh? Trying to get in my pants?" I look down. "I'm not wearing pants."

"Maybe," he says. Smith sets his wine down on his coffee table, next to a large book about boats. I watch him as he takes my wine glass out of my hand and sets it down.

He leans in, and we start kissing feverishly. My mind races as his hands are everywhere, cupping my ass, palming a breast, threading through my hair. Moans echo between our mouths. I deliberately rifle his hair, and he pulls away, panting.

"Should I get a condom?"

I nod like a bobblehead. He jogs away, and I bite my lip as I watch his ass go.

After I unzip the back, awkwardly, I pull my dress off of my shoulders, letting it pool at my feet. A bra doesn't work with this dress so I stand there in my panties and heels. Usually, I would be self-conscious being topless in front of such a huge window, but we're so far up that it's sexy, not scary.

When he comes back, a condom packet pinched between his fingers, he stops in his path.

"My God," he says. He bounds across the space between us, and then I'm in his arms again.

The kisses are hard and frenzied, our breath heavy and labored. I rip the buttons off his shirt to reveal strong abs and I run my fingers down his stomach to cup him.

"Get on my level," I whisper in his ear.

"Yes, ma'am," he says, pulling off his shirt. My mouth waters at his arms, at the Adonis V pointing to his cock. He drops his pants and his boxer briefs, and I cannot tear my eyes away.

Holy shit, his cock is more impressive than I thought.

He spins me around so I'm facing the city, my hands pressed against the glass.

His fingers cup my breast, kneading my nipple as his other hand travels down to between my legs and inside my panties. I gasp as he curves his hand there, the tip of his finger flirting with my opening. I'm still wet from our time in the bathroom, and I ache for him even more.

When his finger dips inside of me, his palm against my clit, I cry out and lean against the window so I don't fall.

"Be as loud as you want to, Cassie," he growls. "No one will hear you scream."

"In another context, that would be creepy."

He laughs the way only powerful men do, his breath tickling my ear. Smith's finger dips lower, finding the soft part within me and presses. I see stars and it mingles with the light of the city. My mouth lets out a deep groan.

"How about now?" he asks.

"Perfect," I say. His hand still in my panties, his other arm wrapped around me, I ride his hand to another orgasm. It breaks me open and I let out a moan as my body settles, slowing his pace.

"Let's go to the bedroom," Smith says in my ear.

"No," I say, hooking my underwear and pushing them down to the ground. "Take me here."

"Alright," he says. I hear rustling as I bend over, planting my hands firmly on the glass. One hand splays on my lower back as he guides his cock with his other.

It feels like paradise. We sigh together and I feel the weight of his chest on my back. As he eases into me, stretching me, he turns my head and kisses me.

"You are spectacular," he whispers in my ear.

Overwhelmed by him inside of me, stretching me, filling me, I say nothing, I just moan. The sensations are too much for me to handle, too much for me to process. I cry out again when he wraps his hand around to touch my clit, his other hand gripping my hip.

Smith thrusts into me, thrumming my walls and making my body pulse with his power.

Smith and I together like this, our connection so hot and all-consuming, is one of the biggest surprises of my life.

It turns from romantic to filthy when our primal instincts take over. His hand goes to my neck and the pleasure overtakes me as I break apart for him and he loses himself too, his breath labored and heavy.

After we settle, he anchors the condom and sits down, butt naked to his couch, the condom still on, his cock still partially erect.

He's breathing hard, his chest rising and falling. He grabs a tissue from his other side table and hands it to me.

I look around, and he senses what I need. He points down the hallway, and I kick off my shoes and run barefoot down his hall. Once I've peed and washed my hands, I look around. Everything is clean and organized, beautifully decorated. I wonder if this was Daniela's doing or he is capable of this himself.

I walk out, and I feel a robe being draped around me.

"That was fun," Smith says, his big hands rubbing up and down the robe sleeves.

"Yes. Definitely."

"Do you want to stay the night?"

My heart constricts. Staying the night seems serious. Yes, he just took me from behind against a huge picture window, and he did go down on me in a bathroom on a boat, but sleeping next to someone, seeing their pillow, how they look while they dream, just feels ten times more intimate to me.

Still I say yes.

He gives me a gray Stanford Law T-shirt that looks like a dress on me. He has a spare, new toothbrush, and when I leave the bathroom to look at his bed, he's placed a glass of water by my side.

"Just in case you get thirsty in the middle of the night," he says.

I climb into bed and into his arms.

In a surprise to no one, we have sex again, this time me on top. At one point, he interlaces his fingers with mine, our hands by his head as I moan. I thought one time would be satisfying, but this time builds on the time before and is even better.

I look down, and his eyes on me, our hands together, just raw and real, is more than anything I ever expected.

He sits up and consumes me, kisses my breasts and my

neck, and I continue to ride his lap, rolling against him, saying his name as I come.

Afterward, I lie there and stare at the ceiling as Smith lightly snores.

HANDS DOWN, the best sex of my life.

Hands down, the most scared I've ever been in my life.

I think Smith is asleep until he says, "I feel like it's okay to say this now, but your 'Girlfriend Soothes You to Sleep' is my favorite video, and I watch it every night to go to bed."

I turn over and I put my hand to his face.

"I'm here so I can give you the real thing," I whisper as my fingernails rake his stubble.

Let's not dwell on the fact that I called myself his girlfriend. Or that this feels natural, like we've been dating for months and this is a typical weekend night. I do not remember that video's script by heart, but I do my best. I whisper, "Baby, I know you've had a long day. Let me pamper you so you fall asleep and get the rest you need."

He kisses me, and damn, is it romantic.

It's also freaking me out.

"This is so nice. Having someone here," he says before he drifts off to sleep.

His eyelashes fluttering with light snores through his nose.

Hours pass, and I get no sleep. My mind will not shut up.

Smith's lonely, like me; he's broken. He just got divorced from a woman who cheated on him, and he is not whole. I'm just some rebound, some crush requited, some ass he finally got after he'd thought about it for too long. It doesn't matter it's me.

All of this will end, no matter if I stay or not. The last

three years of finding myself will be for nothing. This shows I've made zero progress, because I feel myself falling for a man who is raw and vulnerable and will destroy my heart if I let him.

I was weak and needy and powerless when I dated. That same feeling creeps over me like bugs in the springtime as I lie here, with a sexy arm over my stomach.

Around two in the morning, my eyes tugging with exhaustion, I know I need to leave.

I look at Smith, content and asleep. I kiss him on the cheek, and he stirs, but clings to his pillow harder.

After I dress, I avoid the elevator and take the stairs, and my feet are killing me before I reach the lobby. After ordering an Uber, I wait, looking back every so often. I'm not sure why. He wasn't awake when I left and wouldn't know I was gone.

When the Uber pings me to tell me that it's close, I walk outside. The wind whips against my cheeks, and it hits something wet, cooling my skin. My fingers wipe it away, and I stare in disbelief.

Tears.

I breathe in and my nose rattles from the emotion, but I shake it off.

It's better this way.

I get into the car, and the Uber driver confirms my destination. I watch the building drift away, and it tugs at my heart.

The tears really fall as we drive through the city, and I crumple in a ball in my apartment, alarmed that I somehow care so much.

It'll pass. It has to pass.

Smith is not my future.

Not at all.

8

"You did *what*?" Vincent asks, stirring another Stevia packet into his latte.

"I ran out while he was sleeping." I cradle my chai in my hands, unable to look my best friend in the face.

It's a week later, and I've been in a funk since I snuck out of Smith's apartment. I didn't know what I expected. Smith chasing me down after chasing me down once? I made it clear there was no future for us.

It's like it never happened.

It's better this way. I have my friends. I have my YouTube channel.

Still, I'm sad, sitting in this hipster coffee shop with Vincent, one of the loves of my life. Even when we talked about the wedding, how he and his husband had the best time, I cannot force a smile. I feel even more like shit when Vincent looks at me with a knowing look.

He knows as well as I do that I fucked up.

"You are cold," Vincent says. "Was the sex bad? I mean, he's too good-looking. There has to be something wrong with him."

I shake my head. I've never used the term "making love" because ew, gross—but my night with Smith felt like that. And saying he made love to me doesn't make me want to heave.

I'm even thinking about our chat in the elevator and how everything was so easy once my dumb ass realized he wasn't a jerk.

When he admitted to being attracted to me. How it made me feel the most excited I've felt in a while.

I take a sip of my drink. "It's better this way."

Vincent shakes his head. "That's quitter talk," Vincent says, taking a sip of his latte, then making a face. "This fake sugar is slowly crumbling my spirit."

"You look great, though."

Vincent kisses my hand. "We have our honeymoon booked for two months out. Q has an eight-pack, and I do not want anyone looking at me like he settled," Vincent says. He takes another sip and winces.

"I just don't know. I'm not looking to date anyone, and while the sex was amazing..."

"Marry him," Vincent says.

"I can't. First off, he needs to ask."

"Technicality."

"Second, I'm not the type of woman people marry. I'm destined to be single the rest of my life."

"Honey, your worldview is *so* warped." Vincent settles his hands on the table. "Q and I went to couples' therapy so I feel like I'm qualified to deconstruct this."

"Okay." I squirm in my seat.

"Who hurt you?"

I glare at him and tilt my head. "Really? You know about all of it."

"Still," he says with a bob of the head. "Talking it out will help."

I shrug one shoulder. "I moved here with Wade and then he *cheated* on me. I chased my college boyfriend Nate relentlessly and he called me crazy in front of everyone. I've had so many men really excited about me after dates just to ghost me or get back with their ex. Or, claim to not be ready. I've dated carbon copies of Smith and it's never gone well."

I breathe in and out. "Dating and relationships made me miserable and turned me into someone I didn't want to be."

"It's been three years," Vincent says, covering my hand with his. "I think you're cured. You got dicked down better than you have ever been and left in the middle of the night like a boss. You're my hero."

Shaking my head, I say, "I don't know. I thought I was happy being single. But..."

Smith. He ruined it for me.

"You know, I'm not supposed to say anything but Smith asked me about you. Again."

My heart flutters at his name, his interest in me. "He did?"

"You're welcome, by the way. Do you know how hard it was to sleuth out that booze cruise you were on? I had to DM Raegan on Instagram. She's lovely, good job for finding her."

"She is," I say, but all I can think about is Smith. "What did he say?"

"He texted me yesterday. Wondered if I had heard from you."

A slight smile creeps on my face, and Vincent points and says, "A-ha! I knew you weren't an unfeeling bitch."

Vincent is literally the only man who I would ever let call me a bitch.

He takes a sip of his coffee and winces. "I know men

suck sometimes. When Q and I first started to date, I had been burned so many times that I pushed him away. After our fifth, magical date, he had roses delivered. I finally looked myself in the mirror and said, 'Vincent, let that man love you.' And then I did. I've never been happier. I mean, look at this rock."

He flashes his wedding ring, an audacious thick band with diamonds all around. I'm surprised he can hold his hand up.

I pause and look off to the corner of the coffee shop. There was something there with Smith. It was more than amazing sex and I know it, but I'm so scared of what it means.

There might be too much risk for me to stomach.

"What about Daniela?" I bring up. "He was with her for years. and she *cheated* on him. I'm not sure if *he's* ready for a relationship."

"Cassie, dear," Vincent says, waving off. "You wonder where we got the couples' therapist referral from? That marriage was long over before she fell on a dick."

"How long?"

"Years," Vincent says. "They had nothing in common. Daniela liked to be out and around people and Smith is more introverted. If you haven't noticed, the son of a bitch doesn't talk much."

He talks with me.

It makes sense, the difference between Smith and Daniela. I do remember her talking to everyone when she came in, Smith silent with his hand on her back. I can talk to anyone, but I would much rather snuggle on a couch binging something on Netflix than go out any day of the week.

I wonder what Smith is binging right now.

"Are you starting to realize you're self-sabotaging?" Vincent asks, spiral-pointing to my forehead.

I take a sip of my chai. "I am not."

I'm lying. I'm terrified. How maybe I've been lying to myself about men and relationships because it was safer than putting myself out there. How my whole life might turn out differently than I thought with Smith in the picture. But what if it turns out like I thought, but I'll have a huge broken heart to go with it if Smith doesn't stay in the picture?

"Cassie, I love you, but you are lying through those beautiful teeth of yours."

"My girlfriends think I should give him a chance," I say.

"Do it," Vincent says. "It's better to give it a shot than spend your entire life wondering."

"I knew you would have the right thing to say."

"I wouldn't suggest you go after him unless he was worthy of you. And Cassie, you are a goddess."

"Thanks Vincent," I say.

"I got to go, but give me a hug," he says, standing up. He takes me in a bear hug and as he rubs my back, he whispers, "Call him."

"I'll think about it."

As I leave with my purse on my shoulder, he says, "You know, the Octavo is close to here."

I narrow my eyes. "Is this why you suggested this place?"

"Maybe," he says, leaving the coffee shop and disappearing into a sea of people.

I weave in and out of tourists on the Embarcadero, as I end up in front of where it all began.

The Octavo.

It looks different in the daytime, but a warmth goes

through me, although the wind chills my skin. People walk right past me, pretending like I'm not there.

I remember the laughs, the kiss in the elevator. How I was so wrong about him. How he made me feel like he was worth trusting. How he felt different than the other men I've dated.

My hands shake as I unlock my phone, thinking about my two potential futures and what they would look like. There's a good chance that Smith and I might not work out if we tried, but the what-if would kill me. I would spend the rest of my life wondering.

I dial his office number by heart. When I worked for him, Smith's calls were routed to a voicemail box he checked frequently, even on weekends.

I'm shocked when he picks up.

"Hello?"

"Hi, um, it's Cassie," I say.

"Where are you?" Smith asks.

"Funny enough, I'm in front of the Octavo actually."

"Don't move, I'll be right there," he says.

"Okay," I say as the line goes dead.

Fifteen minutes later, he's here and in front of me.

Smith is sweaty, wearing a button-down shirt, stained with perspiration. His hair is damp, and he's breathing heavy. Reminds me of our time in his apartment.

"I didn't think you would be working today."

He coughs against his fist. "Well, I've been monitoring my office line, just in case. Since I don't have your new number."

"Oh," I say.

"I ran here," Smith says.

I look down at him and nod. "I see."

We move to the side so we can talk.

He points to the building. "I've been running by it every day too. In athletic clothes, not this. I've been commenting your videos too."

"What have you been saying?"

Smith looks to the sky. "Some version of 'talk to me.'"

"Oh. I ignore comments like that."

We stand there, quiet.

"I, um..." we both say at the same time. I then laugh and he motions for me to speak.

"I'm sorry I ran out in the middle of the night," I say.

"Was it bad or...?"

"No, no, it was great," I reassure him.

I look down, collecting my words. *Be brave.*

Looking up at him, I say, "I honestly thought I'd be alone forever. However, being with you, being around you..."

"I know," he says. "I didn't think I was ready either. After Daniela."

My heart seizes. "Are you?"

"Yes." No hesitation. No wavering. He peers at me, waiting for a reaction. "I'm absolutely crazy about you. I want to see where this goes."

"Me too. But I'm scared," I say. He's silent, deep in thought. My breath catches in my throat as I wait for his response.

"I am too. But it's worth a shot. With you. How about dinner?" he asks suddenly.

I grin like a fool. "Sounds great."

"Are you available tonight?" he asks. "I know a place that does a mean crab cake."

I wonder who told him of my affinity for crab cakes.

There's no need to play hard-to-get. I nod.

"Great," he says.

Smith leans in tentatively, like he's waiting for me to stop him. He kisses me sweetly, like a first kiss at a middle-school dance.

We both look up at the Octavo together. He slides a tentative arm around my shoulders, and I lean into him.

"You know, I'm grateful that the elevator broke down," Smith says.

"Why?"

"I doubt I would've had the guts to declare my feelings otherwise," Smith says. "I feel like you're out of my league."

I almost drop to my knees on the sidewalk. Me, out of *his* league?

"Stop," I say with a play-slap to his chest. "Were you nervous?"

He nods with a grin. "I've been crushing on you for years, and I was finally single? Oh yeah."

"How much did you like me?"

"So much," he says. "I had to make myself scarce the days you wore your black skirt."

"The pencil skirt?"

"Is that what it was called? It made your ass look amazing."

I nod once. "It was the pencil skirt."

He turns toward me, wrapping his arms around my shoulders. I smell his masculine scent, and I press my cheek into his hard chest. I look up, and he brushes my hair away, framing my face with his hands.

"The elevator breaking down was fate."

"I don't believe in that stuff. Although," I say, looking up into his eyes, "my friend's boyfriend said the same thing, and then he was seated next to her on an airplane."

He brushes hair out of my face. "You might be the Buffy to my Angel."

"Please don't leave me and move to Los Angeles."

"I won't. San Rafael sounds nice, though. But only if you come with me."

"Oh, already talking about the future."

"Not now. But maybe soon."

He leans in again, kissing me, and I wrap my arms around his neck. When I pull away, Smith nods to the hotel.

"Do you want to see if the elevator is free?"

I shake my head violently. "I'll need at least a year before I even go anywhere *near* that elevator."

"Noted," Smith says.

He kisses me again, and I fall under his spell.

God bless weddings, broken elevators, and pushy friends.

EPILOGUE

ONE YEAR LATER

"Where are we going?" I ask, unable to see through the blindfold. Raegan is leading me somewhere by the hand. She's leaving the city so I met her for lunch at one of our favorite spots. We talked about a new murder mystery docuseries I'm obsessed with, and then she proceeded to blindfold me and take me to an unknown location.

At least she didn't put me in the trunk.

"Just because you're leaving doesn't mean you get to kidnap me."

"We're almost there," she says. Raegan's work contract is up, so she's moving back to her hometown next week. I'm devastated.

"Don't you have a date scheduled with Landon's old roommate, Henry?"

"Ugh, yes. We're going to an amusement park next Saturday. Landon and Erin are coming too so it'll be a double date. They know I'm leaving, but they're insisting."

"Maybe Henry is the one."

"I don't know. I saw his picture, and I'm *not* impressed," Raegan said. "And I *do not* like roller coasters."

"You'll be fine. Are we almost there?"

"Yes, just a little bit longer." I shuffle against the floor, careful to not trip. I am definitely in a building, and I hear lots of voices and feel movement around me.

"Okay, take off the blindfold," Raegan says. I pull it down from my eyes.

I'm in the Octavo, and I'm facing the elevator from hell.

Well, at least he waited a year.

My handsome boyfriend stands there, in a black suit with a black tie, holding a bouquet of red roses. His face breaks into a smile, and I know what's coming.

We ended up not moving slow at all. I moved in with him within a month, and we talked about getting married very early in our relationship. He said "I love you" the day I received my Gold YouTube Creator reward in the mail for reaching one million subscribers.

I'm ridiculously, irrationally, insanely in love with him.

Last month, I accidentally found a ring when I was unpacking all of our stuff for the new house. We finally moved out of the city into a small townhome in San Rafael. It already feels more peaceful and tranquil than San Francisco ever was. He's been working from home more than usual and we've had lazy mornings with coffee outside and it's been bliss.

I'm happier than I ever imagined.

Now, he is standing here, in front of me, in our elevator.

I cover my face to hide the emotion, but it's futile. I will be a blubbering mess soon.

"Babe, come here," he says, holding out his hand.

I take it and join him in the elevator. I turn to Raegan and point. "Please make sure this elevator goes nowhere."

"The manager assured me this is going nowhere," she

says, holding her phone up to take video.

I turn toward my love, looking into his gray-blue eyes. We had talked about getting married for so long, but now that it's here, it feels surreal and like it's happening to someone else.

I thought I would never get married. Until I started dating Smith.

It became clear to me almost immediately that I had nothing to worry about. That I could trust Smith with all of me. That he could trust me too. That he would protect me and I would protect him right back.

Smith drops to his knee and pulls out the blue box I found last month.

"Cassandra Renee Gallagher, you are the love of my life. Please marry me and make me the happiest man in the world."

I nod vigorously. He stands up and kisses me, framing my face with his hands like he did with our very first kisses. He wraps his arms around me in a tight hug and lifts me. Being in his arms is my favorite place to be.

"Oh you guys are so cute! Congratulations!" Raegan says, hugging us both. "I'll leave you two alone."

Smith hits a button, and the doors close. I freeze.

"Babe, I'm giving this ring back if you get us stuck in this elevator again."

He laughs and kisses my head. "It's okay. The manager also assured us there's been no malfunction since the night of the wedding. I may have also casually mentioned I could still file a claim and he better be sure."

"Oh, threatening to sue gets me all hot and bothered," I say, kissing him again. I can taste the need in his kiss. I pull away and nod once.

"I love you, Ms. Gallagher."

"I *love* you, Mr. Kennedy."

I smack the stop button of the elevator, halting it. He laughs as he scoops me up and kisses me again, making the world fade away.

THE END

BONUS: WHEN CASSIE LEFT

SMITH

M y vision is cloudy when I wake up the next morning. It feels like a dream at first. My dream girl was in my apartment, and now she's gone. Was she even here?

Her smell clings to the pillow, a soft floral scent, so I know it happened. Flopping onto my back, I scrub my face.

Cassandra Gallagher. Cassie. She was here. I didn't dream it.

Why did she escape? Did I say something that turned her off? Was it too much to share I fell asleep to her videos every night as a consolation prize to talking to her when I had the chance?

I still remember the day she started working for me. The night before, I had stayed up late researching case law for a client, since my last legal secretary quit to go to law school. Her desk had sat empty for months and I had been dragging my feet on hiring a replacement. The thought of training a new person, letting them into my space, learning to trust them—it felt like an insurmountable challenge. One I didn't have the brain capacity for. My marriage was dying a slow death, and it was killing me in the process.

Daniela, my wife at the time, acted like she was asleep when I slipped in, but she wasn't. Her eyes flashed open and mine did too. She poked and poked, saying, *you work too many hours, you don't care about me, you can't ignore me* until the sun came up. Before she drifted off, I heard "I should just leave you. I don't know why I stay" under her breath.

So Cassie's first morning, I walked in, half asleep, a large coffee with two additional shots in my hand to find a blonde sitting in that empty desk. She smiled when I passed her without a good morning and she stood up anyway, following me into my office.

"Hi! You must be Smith. My name is Cassie, pleasure to meet you." She outstretched her hand and my breath hitched. Her eyes lit up brightly; her smile vibrated into me. It threw me off balance. Instead of looking her in the eye, my eyes fell to my organized desk, and I didn't touch her. If just her smile could affect me, what would a brush of hands do?

"Who hired you?" I grumbled. I watched her face fall and I felt like a complete dick.

"Mr. Jones." Her voice is small.

My best friend Quentin has great taste, so I dismiss her with a hand wave.

I knew if I shared one ounce of myself with her, I would regret it. Be a bigger asshole than I already was.

For five years, I ignored her. I held my breath when she walked by me because her scent tempted me. My wife's ring still sat on my finger, although she had moved to the other bedroom.

Then, one day, I arrived home to find no trace of my wife. She had filed for divorce that very day.

When Cassie quit, I saw the hurt in her eyes. I shouldn't have yelled at her. It wasn't her fault my life was falling apart. There were some days seeing her at my desk kept me going. It was something I looked forward to. Then, she was gone, and I spent way too many moments, when I should be working, thinking about her.

Then, Quentin married Cassie's best friend and I saw my chance to make things right.

I couldn't have anticipated how spectacular it went.

The elevator. That *kiss.* Our time in the bathroom on the cruise. Taking her back to my place and sinking into her felt sinful, because I never expected I'd get a chance to. The girl I didn't let myself think about was mine.

For a night anyway. Maybe that's all I deserve.

I search my apartment for a note. Anything. I still don't have her new phone number, so I set my hands on my hips. My laptop sits on my counter, and I swipe it, opening to YouTube and finding Cassie's ASMR channel, Cassie Whispers.

Clicking on the first video, I wasn't prepared for her to pop up. Smiling, her voice low and husky in its whisper, brushing the screen with her fingers. Tingles roll down my arms as I watch and I get lost for a moment, just letting the response hit me, over and over again as I watch the most beautiful girl in the world.

Her blonde hair is half up, her cheeks rosy. Her top is on the lower cut side, so my eyes roam over her collarbone, the curve of her neck, the light freckles across her chest. My lips touched that last night; I had her breasts in my hands, her nipple in my mouth.

I contemplate walking away, letting her disappearance be my answer.

However, if there's one thing that my failed marriage and

my time as a lawyer has taught me—don't give up, not even a little bit.

I scroll to the comment section. My Youtube account has a gray avatar, so I pick a headshot of mine and update it. I change my username to Smith C. Kennedy, so there's no doubt it's me.

My fingers freeze over the keypad. What do I say? It must have an impact. She has so many admirers, there's a lot of creeps. She may still skirt past my comment or may not see it at all.

I have to try.

In the end, I decide on the simple. *Please talk to me.*

A variation of this comment goes on several videos: I'm concentrating on the new ones. It's spammy, but I don't care. If I said anything last night that made her think I didn't want her there, that I wasn't ready to see where this goes, I need to make it as clear as ice.

I want her. So badly.

Six days pass, and nothing. I sink myself in work, pulling twelve-hour days so my mind doesn't drift. My ringer has been on for the first time in seven years, but every time it dings, my hopes lift just to come crashing to the ground. My comments on her videos have slowed since it's clear she doesn't see them or she's ignoring them.

I go for long runs, passing by the Octavo, hoping she'd be pulled there like me.

My secretary knows to interrupt me immediately if she gets a call from Cassie Gallagher.

Still nothing.

I have one last resort.

Her best friend, Vincent, was a great source before, finding out from her friend she'd be on the booze cruise, the one I crashed, and we did what we did in the bathroom. And then, I had the best night of my life just to wake up to a cold bedside.

I send the text before I can talk myself out of it.

Me: Vincent, how are you man?

The bubble with the dots happen immediately.

Vincent: Hey, how are you? Did you find Cassie?

A smile crosses my lips thinking about our night almost a week ago.

Me: I did.

The dots appear and then disappear. I don't know what to say.

Vincent: And?

How do I say this? It's not gentlemanly to kiss and tell.

Me: It went well.

Vincent: I'm glad to hear it.

Me: Thank you for your help.

Immediately, Vincent texts me back.

Vincent: Why are you texting me then?

My heart thumps in my chest.

Me: She rushed out of here.

Vincent: What?

Vincent: Ooooooohhhhh

Me: Have you heard from her?

Vincent's face fills my phone as it rings, an atrocious synthesized song that hurts my ears. I need to change it.

"Hello?"

"Bro, what did you do?"

"I didn't do anything," I say. "I didn't want her to leave."

"I'll get to the bottom of this. But she's my best friend, Smith, and I don't care how strong you are or how still scared I am of you from working at the firm. If you hurt her, I swear to God..."

"I didn't! We had a lovely time and I thought she would stay, and she didn't. I don't have her phone number."

Vincent breathes in and out. "She does this. Leave it to me. If she hears from you, it's because she wants to. I have no control over this, Smith. She's ran away from you twice. I'm only doing this because you got us the KitchenAid mixer."

A deep whoosh of breath leaves my lips. "Thank you, man."

"You're welcome. But I do recommend giving up if you don't hear from her. It might not be meant to be."

I'm not crazy; I know what happened. It was the best sex of my life, and I can't make up that kind of connection. It was special and rare. Right?

"Please, just talk to her."

"I'll text her right now. But, Smith, please…"

"I'll give up if I don't hear from her. Just don't tell her we talked more than the text."

"Okay," Vincent says.

"Vincent, Cassie is…everything. I care about her. A lot."

"I know." The line goes dead.

When the phone rings the next day, I'm writing notes from a case file, and I answer. I've been working every day on the off chance she'll call the office line. It's usually a client who didn't expect to get me, so I give a "hello?" as I continue to write.

"Hi, um, it's Cassie," she says.

It's her. It's really her. I drop my pencil and grip the phone so hard next to my face, it hurts.

"Where are you?"

"Funny enough, I'm in front of the Octavo actually."

I do a quick estimation—the hotel is about a mile and a

quarter from my office. I'm in dress clothes but I don't care. "Don't move, I'll be right there."

"Okay," she says.

The elevator is taking too long so I take the stairs. I tear out, in the direction of the hotel. I dodge tourists and homeless camps and when I get to the Octavo, I search the crowd.

Please still be here.

Then, the crowds part and there she is.

She looks like an angel.

There's dampness under my arms as I approach her. It's been a long time since I've felt this afraid, but this is worth it.

She is worth it.

I hope she can't hear the large lump I just swallowed as I wait for her to speak.

For Your Safety

1

An avalanche of water pours over my date's head.

"Oh my God, look at you! You got *nailed*!" an obnoxious thirteen-year-old yells at Henry with a cackle and a finger point. Henry says nothing as the teenager's best friend starts in on the mockery and points at him too. My date Henry, a grown-ass man, does nothing.

Say something, point at the teenagers too, *something.*

Since there's only four of us, Henry and me on a double-date with my friend Erin and her fiancé Landon, we're stuck with two random middle schoolers on this six-person water raft ride. The children sat down, already soaking wet, and it's clear they're cycling through the line like men cycle through online dating profiles.

The children mimic Henry's shocked face the minute the waterfall took him over, and he blushes. No quick remark, no witty comeback, nothing.

I make a mental note of yet another reason Henry is not my forever.

Frankly, this date was doomed from the start. When my friend Erin sent me a picture of Henry, I was underwhelmed. Henry has cropped strawberry-blond hair, pale skin, and light eyes—not my usual type at all.

When we met outside the theme park for the first time, I zoned in on the suburban-dad white tennis shoes with black socks hiked up to halfway on his hairy calves. Even though he's the same height as me, he didn't look me in the eye.

I'm typically attracted to taller men with darker hair and a poet's soul.

So, when we shook hands, I felt nothing. Not a blip. Not a single zing.

It's for the best, actually. This is my last weekend before I move home, and I don't need anything complicating that move. I've already cried *a lot* about leaving San Francisco. I don't need another reason to cry.

I cry at everything already.

Erin and her fiancé Landon suggested this double-date to Thrill Mountain, an amusement park on a flat piece of land on the outskirts of San Francisco County as a way for Henry and me to meet. I don't really like amusement parks, but I've made a habit of saying yes.

Yes to a sixteen-month contract in my dream city, San Francisco.

Yes to getting a tattoo on my wrist because my friend was getting one too.

Yes to a date I don't think is going to go anywhere when I'm leaving town in two days.

This meeting almost didn't happen, but Henry just returned to San Francisco from a year-long residence in Singapore. Erin constantly insisted Henry and I are perfect for each other.

"I just wish he would come home so you could meet," she would say over brunch or our wine-and-charcuterie nights. "You would be great together. You have so much in common."

I don't know about you, but I take no shit from middle schoolers.

The raft ascends another apex, through rock formations and foliage. The children vibrate with sugar and screams of excitement.

Henry's eyes bug at the next climb, and I notice his Adam's apple bob and his lips part.

Yep, nothing going on downstairs for me. Not even a flicker.

"I'm sure this boat will spin, and they'll get it this time," I say with my brightest smile as my date looks terrified.

"I hope so," he says. "My balls are in my stomach right now."

I gasp out a laugh at the randomness from him. I did not expect jokes from a man who got nauseous on the Spinster and dry-heaved into the corner for five minutes.

When we reach the top, the teenagers scream for no reason before we even drop, startling me in my seat. "Here we go!" one of the boys says as we crest the top and the raft sails down the drop while twisting, and a wave of water covers the two boys we're sharing the boat with.

Sweet, sweet revenge.

"Haha," I say with a finger point to them. The water gives them power since one shakes off droplets and yells like he just conquered an army in a battle while the other laughs maniacally like a demon child.

"I'm so scared of them," Henry whispers.

"Don't be," I whisper. "They're just kids. Let's have fun with them."

I turn to them and yell, "You *got* nailed!"

Turning toward Henry, I say, "See, not so scary."

"You're going let your girlfriend stick up for you?" one teenager says to Henry as water drips down his chin.

Blood drains from my face. Maybe middle schoolers *are* scary. "I'm not his girlfriend," I object.

"Did you get friend-zoned, bro?" one of them asks, and Henry's pale skin flushes under the water droplets.

"Man, kids are brutal these days," Erin mutters to herself.

"No shit," Landon adds.

I open my mouth to speak, but Henry leans in, his proximity doing nothing. "Please. Make them stop. I will have nightmares about this for weeks."

I laugh nervously, not sure if he's joking or not. This is the most Henry has talked to me this whole date.

"They're egging you on. Don't you want to stick up for yourself?" I ask.

"No. I prefer to sit in my misery and cold clothes," he says.

Negative. Another point off for Henry Mansfield.

It's an agonizing few minutes until we reach the rotating wood deck, and we unbuckle our seatbelts to get off the damp ride. The teenagers disappear immediately.

"We got out relatively unharmed. Except for Henry's ego," Erin says to me, wrapping an arm around my shoulders. "Poor Henry."

We watch Henry step out, the water dripping from his cargo shorts.

"I need to talk to you," I say, grabbing Erin's hand.

Erin turns to the men. "We're going to hit the ladies'."

"I'm going to sit in the sun to dry off and get heat stroke," Henry says, and Landon laughs as he smacks him on the back.

We find a bathroom near an arcade and walk in. I turn toward Erin with crossed arms.

"You bamboozled me," I say.

"Come again?" Erin asks, her face blank.

"Henry. I don't see what we have in common at all. He barely talks, and he's not having a good time, not in the least."

"Look," Erin says. "Henry is a *little* awkward, but he's a really good guy. I promise. There is something there..."

"I don't feel anything with him. No spark. Plus, I'm moving literally Monday."

"I refuse to accept that you're moving. To your other point, I think the spark is overrated. Your picker is off. What about the last guy whose poetry reading you dragged us to? His poetry was *awful,* and I wanted to punch him."

"Kelvin," I say.

"Was his real name Kevin?"

"I never confirmed, but probably."

I fell for Kelvin's guitar-playing and man bun, his passion for minimalism and sustainable living. He knew I was fluent in French, and he would string random vocabulary words in a terrible accent to make me laugh.

Ultimately, the angst of our relationship drove me crazy, and he eventually blocked my number.

Erin and our other friend Cassie—who recently got engaged to her boyfriend Smith—listened to me rant and cry about dating in San Francisco one too many times. The men here are either gay or drive me crazy.

But it's the reason I'm here at an amusement park, something I'm not a big fan of, on a date with a guy I have no future with.

"Leave no stone unturned" is my new dating mantra.

At the very least, I get to spend time with Erin before I leave.

She's lucky I love her when she says, "I think we're heading to the Double Helix next."

I freeze and swallow the lump in my throat.

The showcase roller coaster of the theme park, The Double Helix. My hands shake thinking about riding it. Dread prickles my temples, and I place a hand on the tiled wall.

Besides being afraid of heights, I've been scared of roller coasters ever since I was eight, when I crashed my older sister's slumber party and they were watching *Final Destination 3*. A roller coaster accident happens in the first ten minutes, and the main character's boyfriend being split in half still haunts my memories.

"Stop looking so pale, it'll be fun," Erin says, grabbing my hand and pulling me out of the bathroom. "And fall in love with Henry, please. So you'll stay."

"Don't get your hopes up." We tumble out of the bathroom and find Landon and Henry.

"Double Helix?" Erin asks. Landon's face brightens, and he envelops his fiancée.

"I can't wait!" Landon shouts excitedly.

Henry and I wear matching "I'm about to throw up" expressions.

"Are you nervous?" I whisper to Henry.

"Yes. You?"

"Yes."

"They're not going to let us get out of it," Henry says.

"I don't think so," I agree.

"Well, at least we'll be in this together." He smiles, and for the first time, I feel a tiny bond form between us.

At least this date won't be totally heinous.

"Let's get this over with," I say as we head toward the Double Helix.

We round a corner of gift shops to see the monstrosity. I hear the movement of the trains and the screams as we get closer, and I shake out my hands.

The Double Helix is a bright-green ride with huge drops and two loops and a few corkscrews. Its claim to fame is two tracks intertwining way too close to one another to possibly be safe. We pass under it, and Henry and I look up at the same time. We look at each other with similar terror in our eyes.

I'm determined to be a good date and face this fear. I've done far scarier things. I lived by myself in France for a year. I moved to San Francisco on my own. I found a mouse in my apartment.

This is nothing. I will be fine.

Erin and Landon pause at the entrance so we can join them. We let four teenagers go ahead of us, and we weave in between the metal barricades to come to a halt.

"Doesn't look like that long of a line," Landon says, peering over the crowd. He pulls Erin to him, her back pressed against his front, his arms looped around her waist.

My heart squeezes. Watching Erin plan her wedding to the man of her dreams makes me realize how much I want that. I haven't met a man yet who makes me feel the way I imagine Erin feels. Or Cassie feels. Over a year of dating in San Francisco was a complete bust for me. I've been dating since I was sixteen. Where the fuck is he?

Maybe once I settle down and ignore my wanderlust, I'll find him.

Henry looks at Landon and Erin and back at me. I freeze. He doesn't expect to cuddle, does he? I cross my arms tightly across my chest so he doesn't get any ideas.

Henry and I study the safety video like we're Elle Woods studying for the LSAT.

"For your safety, keep your arms and legs inside the train at all times," an animated DNA strand says, holding a pointer to a chalkboard with a gloved hand. We wind around, and we're about to go to the bay to be loaded onto the ride.

Now that we're here, I'm freaking out. Everything is a haze. My heart thunders in my chest. I see the exit for chickens right there, an elevator that brings you to the exit for the ride, mixing in with the off-loaded riders, where you feel like a loser for walking off.

"Look," I say to Henry with an inconspicuous point to the lines below. There are our drenched teenage nemeses, climbing into an empty train. "If they're not scared, why should we be scared, right?"

I giggle nervously. Those teenagers would probably *love* it if it goes off the tracks.

"I'm not scared," Henry says, giving a nervous laugh. His smile falls. "Actually, I'm terrified."

"Me too," I say, relaxing.

"We don't have to go on it, you know," Henry counters. "We can just go eat cotton candy and people-watch."

"No," I say with conviction. "How's your stomach?"

"I've felt like throwing up this entire time, so what's one more high-velocity jolt to really reject all of the food I've eaten in the past twenty-four hours?"

I laugh again. Henry might be *funny*? In a dry, self-deprecating way?

We walk down the final staircase to the lines. An employee in a blue jumpsuit is separating guests to his left and right to load on both sides of the dock. He asks the two groups in front of us for the number in their party.

Then he looks up the staircase and holds up a peace sign. "Party of two, party of two?"

"We are!" Henry yells.

I lean in. "We're a party of four," I say. Something about being separated from Landon and Erin terrifies me more.

"We need to get this over as soon as possible," Henry says. "Like ripping off a bandage. Then, we can find a nice bench and stay there until Landon and Erin want to leave."

"You have a point." I say. I hold up the matching peace sign. "Party of two!"

Henry follows me as I pass Erin and Landon, as well as the teenagers and a group of four CSU Hayward students. The employee guides us to the set of seats of a train.

"Okay, we're in this together," Henry says. "We will both scream, and then it will be over and we'll have an ugly keepsake photo to remember it."

"Sounds like a plan," I say.

He turns toward me. "I do have an offer."

"What's that?"

"I can hold your hand. You know, if you get scared," he says.

"Sure," I hear myself say. Holding hands would not be leading him on; it's just solidarity between us. He winks at me as we're coaxed into our seats by an employee.

After we're strapped in and we lower our harnesses, Henry offers an open palm, and I cover his hand with mine. I feel a tiny zing when our fingers intertwine.

2

I'm teetering on the edge of a heights freak-out; it *can't* be sparks of chemistry.

"Wow, you might break my hand," Henry says, looking down at our joined hands. My knuckles are turning white.

"I'm a little nervous," I say. My mouth is dry as my plants' soil at home, so I smack my lips together so I can swallow.

"It would be an honor to have my hand broken by you," he says.

"Oh really?" Is he flirting?

"However, the minute we go over the first hill, I'm dropping your hand and holding onto these handlebars for dear life, just so you know," he says. His eyes jerk to the silver handlebars on the bright green drop harness.

"Fair," I reply. His hand feels nice in mine for the time being.

We sit on the track for an eternity, as the employees check seatbelts and harnesses by pulling and jiggling. Finally, one employee waves his hand down to signal to the person in the control booth. The train starts to move, and I squeeze my eyes shut.

"Why are you closing your eyes? Don't you want to see the crash before your death?"

I laugh out loud. That joke might not work on everyone, but it works on me.

"Why are we doing this?" I ask.

"Our friends are pushy as fuck," Henry says.

We curve around a corner and are faced with the first ascent of the ride. The gears click into place as the train begins its climb and other passengers shriek in excitement.

"This is horseshit," Henry says. "I shouldn't have let Landon talk me into this."

I wonder if he means the date or the ride. Maybe both.

"Oh my God, oh my God, we're really moving," I say. "Oh, fuck. Oh, *fuck*."

"I have too many control issues for this," Henry says. He lets out a scream, his lips stretched across his teeth, and I match his scream, our eyes locked.

His eyes are the color of a fresh-water lake, like the one near my hometown. They're really pretty, actually.

The people directly in front of us flinch. The confusion floats off of them. It's cathartic to let a scream out, but I'm still shaking. The train climbs higher and higher, and my heart drops to my butt.

The train slows and then completely...stops.

Is this normal? Do the roller coaster design people do this to torment people like me?

"What the *fuck*," I yell with an edge of whine.

"Yeah, what the fuuuuuuuuccccccckkkkkk," Henry yells.

Other passengers match our freak out and raise us blind rage.

Henry drops my hand to clench his handlebars.

Against my better judgment, I look behind me and pray that we don't go backward. We are stupid high up. Gasping for air, I close my eyes. Maybe the roller coaster will tip over. Or will start back up again and go too slow over the first hill and then we won't have enough momentum to go through the first loop and then I'll fall out because the harnesses malfunction like in *Final Destination 3* as a giant metaphor of what going back to my hometown feels like to me.

I'm going to die today. Or pass out from the adrenaline crash of a full-blown panic attack.

Without warning, I burst into tears.

Full-on ugly crying, mascara-streaking sobbing that turns into hyperventilating.

I usually reserve crying for the third date.

Henry tenses next to me. "Oh no."

Crying turns into sobbing. There are no stakes to this date, so I let the snot flow and the full ugly-cry manifest enough to make even the most secure man feel uncomfortable.

When I cry, my nose goes up my face, and my mouth stretches into the shape of a jellybean. My nose drains portions of my brain until I'm a shiny and wet mess.

"I hate this," I say with a wail.

Another person begins crying, and then it's a chain reaction. Soon, the whole roller coaster is feeling feelings about being stuck at the first ascent.

The seat's speaker near my ear crackles on.

"Hey, folks! Sorry we stopped! Just hang tight, and we'll get you going in no time!"

"Great, now they're going to start it with no warning," I say, sniffing snot back into my head. "I was barely holding it together back there."

"This is my worst nightmare," Henry says. His hands

cling to the handlebars. "I really need to stop listening to Landon."

"I'm sorry you're stuck here with me." I look down and start sobbing again.

"No, you're the best part about this day," Henry says.

My tears dry immediately. Me?

"You've barely talked to me, though."

"You make me nervous!" he says, rubbing his palms on his shorts. "When I say I don't date, I mean it's been over a year. The only girl I've talked to really is the AI I created on my computer, and oh my God, why did I admit that? I swear it's not creepy, I just..."

"It's fine," I say, my voice cracking from the cry fest earlier. "I've seen *Her*."

"Mine is not like that, I swear. I tried to make a joke. Oh God, oh God, this is middle school all over again." Henry rubs a palm against his shorts.

"You created a dating app, though," I point out. Landon and Henry recently sold the dating app, Kindred, but still concoct projects together. I used their app a few times, with mixed results.

"Yeah, but it was Landon's idea. I just coded it," Henry says. "I tried to use it to get an idea of the interface, but got so overwhelmed, I relied on my beta testers instead."

Overwhelmed by dating and created a robot girl to talk to. Wow.

"Awww, why can't I be cool?" Henry asks, his voice cracking. "Oh, because I'm stuck on this fucking roller coaster."

"Seriously," I say, "I do think I have you beat as the worst half of this date. I'm covered in snot..." I trail off. "I might cry again."

"I'm so nauseous right now." He drums on the handlebars. He reaches awkwardly into his pocket and hands over a tissue. "Here."

"Thanks," I say. I dab at my nose awkwardly.

"You're welcome," Henry says. He breathes in harshly through his nose and lets out a huge exhale. "I can't throw up in front of you. You are literally the prettiest girl I've ever seen. You have these mesmerizing eyes, and your hair..."

I blush and a tiny smile crosses my lips. My hair gets a lot of attention since I've been dyeing it different colors since I was twenty-one. Currently it's "mermaid hair," a combination of green, blue, purple, and pink. One Saturday night, I had nothing to do so I came up with this.

"You think I'm pretty?" I ask. A warm feeling spreads through my chest.

"Absolutely," he says, shaking his hands.

Men tell me some version of this often, but it feels different coming from Henry. It has no sordid intentions, it's just...sweet.

"When's the last time you had a girlfriend?" I ask.

Henry buzzes his lips and huffs out like a horse. "Right before I left for Singapore."

"Why did you break up?"

Henry squints one eye. "The sex was so good, she had to quit. Too sore."

Cackling, my eyes fill up with tears from laughter. Flashes of Henry and me kissing flit across my mind, but I think nothing of it. It's mere curiosity.

Henry looks forward. "I was leaving for Singapore, and we broke up."

"You didn't want her to come with you?"

Henry shakes his head. "She had a life here with a job she really loved. I couldn't ask her to give that all up when I didn't feel the way you're supposed to feel."

"And what's that? The way you're supposed to feel?"

Henry's gaze locks with mine. "Magic."

His word and look glide over my skin, causing goosebumps. I know what he means. There were plenty of times I've should've felt a certain way, but I didn't. Funny, I've completely forgotten about being trapped in a contraption that could fall off or slide backward. My heart rate has slowed, and I'm no longer shaking.

"Long distance is hard too," Henry says. "I've done it before and it's more trouble than it's worth."

Huh.

"Are you from around here?" I ask.

"Healdsburg, born and raised," he says.

I light up. "We go there all the time as a home base for wine tasting."

"I can't think of a better place," he says.

"I freaking love Healdsburg," I say, tapping his hand with my finger. He looks down at where I touched him.

Henry smiles, and his skin grows pink. "It's the best."

"It reminds me of home," I say.

"Where are you from?"

"Goldheart," I say. "It's near Grass Valley and Nevada City..."

"I know where that is. I've been there a couple times," Henry says. "Is your family still there?"

I nod. "My dad and my mom. And my older sister Annie works for a winery there."

"Why did you leave?" Henry asks.

There it is. His gaze making me nervous again.

"I've always loved San Francisco. Been, like, obsessed. I knew I needed to live here before I die."

I left out how my San Francisco adventure was coming to a close, that there was no way I could stay. Even if the tech start-up had kept me, my salary was barely enough to share my portion of the rent with a roommate. San Francisco was only supposed to be temporary so I could get it out of my system.

However, leaving San Francisco is a lot harder than I thought it would be.

Being on top of this roller coaster has made me realize some things.

"I don't know if Erin and Landon told you, but I'm leaving San Francisco," I say.

Henry looks down with a blank expression. Is he sad or indifferent?

"Why?" he asks.

"The city is so expensive."

Henry nods vigorously.

"I had a contract for my current job, but it's over," I say.

"You can't find another job?" he asks.

"No, I haven't really looked. And all the men don't like me. Well, the straight ones," I say.

"Come on," Henry says. "No way."

"Way. I've tried everything. Apps, blind dates, walking up to men in Trader Joe's..." I say.

"Do you go for the same frozen orange chicken bag, hoping for a hand graze?"

"Exactly," I say. "That orange chicken they do is so good, though."

Henry's eyes roll back in his head. "Right? Their egg rolls are pretty good too."

"I haven't tried those."

"You have to," Henry says.

I have a flash of a Trader Joe's frozen Chinese food date with Henry. I wonder what his apartment looks like. I wonder what he's like in bed...

Wait, what am I thinking? Henry is not an option. He certainly doesn't look like my usual type. He's not brooding or tall with my typical preference of dark hair and dark eyes.

I'm leaving, for crying out loud.

I accidentally look over the edge, and my heart rate speeds up again.

"What's wrong?" Henry asks.

"I just looked over the edge. It's so far down. Why is this ride still stuck?"

On cue, the intercom near my ear comes alive again.

"Okay, folks, the Thrill Mountain technicians are hard at work to get the ride up and going for you. It'll be just a few more moments."

"Someone's getting fired today," Henry says.

"So fired," I repeat. I grip the handles on the harness tightly. Being up here with Henry isn't so bad. It's certainly not the worst date I've ever been on, even with Henry's nausea, then the wave assault on the water ride, then the roller coaster crapping out. He's definitely the nicest guy I've been out with in a while. It's like straight single men know they have the upper hand in San Francisco.

Still, I don't feel the twisting of my stomach, any heat between my legs. No desire to grab his face and bruise his lips with mine. He's simply become a friend I've gotten to know while trapped on this ridiculous roller coaster.

"I'm glad I got stuck. With you," I blurt out.

"You are?" Henry asks.

"It hasn't been so bad."

"Oh, can I put that as a blurb on my dating profile? You know, when I'm not overwhelmed?" Henry asks with a raised eyebrow.

"Absolutely. Raegan, former date, says..."

"No, it will read: 'Not bad' – Raegan, former date."

"Perfect," I say as my stomach drops. He's already discounting a future date. I'm not sure why I'm sad.

"Friends?" Henry asks, holding up his right hand. I can't meet it with my right due to my harness, but I link his hand with my left hand in the best shake we can do. It's friendly and reminds me of holding hands as kids.

"Friends," I say with a plastered-on smile.

In that moment, I feel a swell in my chest. It hits me like the water balloon I took to the face at the Goldheart Community Picnic when I was twelve.

Holy shit.

I think I kind of like him.

3

I've had many crushes in my life. There's the Finch brothers in Goldheart, all too good-looking for their own good. There was Jeremy Tanner in middle school who I never talked to and just crushed on from afar. I've had crushes on dates that went nowhere.

None of them looked like Henry. None of them made me laugh like Henry.

I rip my hand away from Henry's, and we both settle our hands on our handlebars. Declaring we were friends cut off all our banter, and I can't think of a good topic to start it up again.

Do I tell him I'm interested?

No, too forward.

Is *he* even interested? Sneaking glances at Henry, I notice he looks ahead with a blank expression. I'm not sure how he feels now that we declared ourselves as friends, when he called me pretty earlier.

I'm losing my mind, sitting here. Have I been way too shallow this whole time? Were a million Henrys under my nose, and I never noticed?

Henry is not my usual type at all. He's a coder, successful, goofy, caring, but also gets motion-sickness and refuses to stand up to teenagers. I never thought I'd date a man who had red hair, but here we are.

My thought spiral is interrupted by an aggravated scream.

"What was that?" Henry asks. We both lift our butts off the seats to try to see.

"This is all your fucking fault, Josh. I told you we should've gone on the Ferris Wheel instead."

Ooooooh, drama.

"I asked you if this was okay! You could've said no!"

"Josh, we've been dating for five years. You should know by now that I *hate* roller coasters. Detest them."

Henry leans in. "I've been dating you for five seconds, and I know you don't like them." My chest swells. *He's dating me.*

Stop it, Raegan. He just said you were friends. Plus, you're leaving. He doesn't do long-distance.

"This is the first time I'm hearing about this, Diana. You have literally never told me you hate roller coasters."

"Well, I also don't really orgasm. How do you like that, Josh? All of our new friends on the Double Helix here know now. Josh does not give me ORGASMS!"

The whole train gasps.

Henry and I turn towards each other. "I'm one hundred percent invested in this," I say.

"Same," Henry says. "I feel like a big bombshell is coming."

"A bigger one than him not giving her orgasms?"

"What about all that moaning last night? You screamed my name so loud the cops got called. They handcuffed me, Diana."

"Yeah, well, you got out, didn't you?" Diana asks. "You weren't even booked."

"Since I asked to speak to my attorney."

Henry turns to me. "Smart. That's how people get in trouble in the true crime shows. I'm always like, 'ask for your attorney, idiot.'"

"Yes!" I say. "You like true crime shows?"

"Unfortunately, yes. I find them soothing."

"Me too." Another point for Henry.

Diana and Josh are back to fighting so we listen in.

"I *knew* I should've hooked up with Wyatt when I had a chance. Now we're stranded on this fucking roller coaster because you wanted to feel the wind on your face."

"Who's Wyatt?" I ask Henry.

"I think we'll find out soon," Henry whispers.

"Wyatt?" Josh asks. "My best friend, Wyatt? When did you almost hook up?"

"It's his best friend," Henry scream-whispers.

"I got it," I say with a wink. Henry's lips straighten, and our eyes lock. He looks down and then back up, and my chest flutters.

Our first moment.

Maybe we can be more than friends. I could drive back to San Francisco and...

No, Raegan. Just because a guy is nice to you doesn't mean he's willing to drive a hundred miles every weekend one way to see you.

I shift in my seat.

"Candice's bonfire. Wyatt and I had the best *time*. He danced with me, which you *never* do."

"I love dancing," Henry tells me. "Even though I'm terrible at it. Lots of flailing arms, lots of tongue past my lips, but you can't drag me off the dance floor. Once I get started. Electric slide, cha-cha slide, give me all the slides."

"You're a much better man than Josh," I say.

"Eons, lightyears ahead of Josh."

I've been Diana at weddings, bringing a guy like Josh who sits in the corner on his phone who refuse to dance with me. It makes no sense to me why men turn down dancing. Seventy-five percent of my dancing technique is pressing my ass against a man's frontside and shimmying. You can usually see right down my dress and most of my favorite ones require me to go braless.

Our new friend Josh has had enough.

"I can't believe you, Diana," Josh says.

"Well, I've been unhappy with you for a long time. When was the last time you went down on me, Josh? When?"

"Oh, Josh," Henry says. "You've got to keep the tongue game strong, my friend."

An ache manifests between my legs at Henry's comment. I've had sex semi-recently, but it included fumbling of clothes with no warm-up time before a dick was inside of me. Henry would take his time, be thorough—I can just tell.

I'm officially curious.

"Diana, I've told you. I hate the way it tastes."

"And cum tastes like a milkshake? Kelis lied to us!"

Preach, Diana, preach.

I also gasp, because I saw at least three children walk onto the roller coaster. While this is hilarious, I don't need it on my conscience that I didn't say something to a couple having a wildly inappropriate personal conversation. I open my mouth to say something, but Henry beats me to it.

"Okay, that's enough, this is getting annoying," Henry

says just to me. He raises his voice. "Hey, how about you keep that to yourself, okay? There's kids on the ride."

"Who said that? Mind your own fucking business."

"It's hard for me to mind my business when you and your girlfriend are airing your dirty laundry, my friend."

"Fuck you, dude."

"Fuck you...harder. Unlike your girlfriend," Henry says. He lowers his voice, and it's only meant for me. "Oh, that didn't come out right. And I'm no better than Josh."

"Maybe I should be with a man like that, Josh," Diana says.

No, maybe I should be with a man like that, Diana.

Josh makes a sound, and Diana lowers her voice, still arguing, but quiet enough that we cannot hear.

My mouth agape, I turn to him.

"What?" he asks.

"You stood up to a guy who sounds like he could kick your ass."

"They were getting out of line."

"What about the middle schoolers?"

"Totally different thing. The kids were just being kids," Henry says. "Plus, I've been deathly afraid of middle schoolers since I was in middle school. Josh and Diana are just idiots. I let the f-word slip, so not my finest moment, but...it had to be said."

There's fire in those pupils. I bite my lip as I study his jawline. It's very nice.

"Oh my God, someone's coming," Henry says. I look down to see a portly man in a blue jumpsuit walking up the stairs adjacent to the track. He passes us, holding onto the railing for dear life with a bullhorn in his dangling hand. When he reaches halfway between the seats, he puts the bullhorn to his lips.

"We appreciate your patience, ladies and gentlemen. We will begin the evacuation shortly. I'm just waiting for some of my colleagues to join me."

"*Evacuation*?" I ask, alarmed. Looking down, I see the flimsiest stairs, with slats that I could easily trip going down, and I swear the banister is held together by spit and duct tape.

Henry and I look at each other with long, terrified faces. I'm not sure what's more terrifying—the ride itself or evacuating off the ride.

"I completely forgot we're a million stories in the air," Henry says. "They're going to undo my harness, and I'm going to be *asked to stand up* and walk down those stairs. Look at me. Do I look like a man who is coordinated when he's nervous?"

"I'll catch you if you fall." I look over the edge again and shake my head. "Wait, no, I won't. Sorry, Henry, you may be on your own. I'll be amazed if I don't hyperventilate."

"You and me both," Henry says. "I psyched myself up for a date, not a death-defying stunt of walking down stairs."

"We're a mess."

"A hot mess," he agrees.

"Why did we agree to this?"

"Because we're pushovers, that's why," Henry says. "You know what we need to do if ever we get off this ride?"

"What?"

"We have to ditch Landon and Erin. Before we're convinced to go on another ride that breaks down that we didn't want to go on in the first place."

"Yeah?"

"Full-on stuff our faces with cotton candy and beer and sit on a park bench and people-watch. You can't get stuck on rides if you don't go on them."

"You want to keep hanging out with me? The crying didn't scare you off?" I ask. "I straight-up *sobbed*."

"I grew up with three sisters. I'm used to emotions," Henry says. "Your crying episode does not even register on the top five cries I've witnessed. You look really pretty when you cry. Ugh, I didn't mean it that way...uh..."

My heart pitter-patters. "I always thought I ugly-cried."

"No, no, no," Henry says. "Your eyes get red around the center, but it makes them look really green. Like emeralds."

That could be a cheesy line coming from any of the several app-trolling douchebags I've gone on a date with in the past few months. From Henry, it makes my insides melt like hot fudge.

Without warning, Henry grabs my hand, and I look down at it. Hot fireworks shoot up my arm, and I smile at him. His face breaks, and he's smiling too.

Maybe he wants to be more than friends.

I'm not sure if I should say it. If proclaiming it out loud would jinx it or make it untrue.

What the hell.

"If we make it off of this ride, I'm going to lay one on you."

"Lay a punch?"

"No," I say with a giggle.

"Lay a lei?" Henry asks.

I shake my head again.

"Lay a...kiss?" Henry asks. His lips curl up in a boyish smirk, and the butterflies have arrived. They were a little delayed, but now, they're flapping and dive-bombing in my stomach and I can't stop smiling.

"Yes. A big, fat juicy one. If you're okay with it, of course."

"I should've remembered my Binaca," he says, and I

laugh, imaging him pausing me so he could spray some breath freshener in his mouth.

"You didn't expect I would want to kiss you?"

"No," Henry says. "You're way too pretty. I thought there was no way."

"I think you're pretty cute," I say. When I start involuntarily flirting, it's definitely a good sign.

"Please," he says. "I know what I am. I'm a six at best if I was broke. App money bumps me up to about a seven and a half."

"Stop," I say, laughing. The self-deprecating humor is killing me. All this time, I focused on how a guy looked in a suit or what kind of car he drove. Who knew a guy wearing black socks and white tennis shoes would work for me? A guy who hates heights as much as I do, who gets as nauseous and nervous on roller coasters as I do. A guy who likes to dance, just because.

I was so busy focusing on a guy's look, that I didn't ever wonder about their heart.

"Do you want to kiss me?" I ask.

Henry let out a *phew* sound from his mouth. "Of course."

"Good," I say. Henry squeezes my hand three times, and I pause. That was something my dad does whenever I'm nervous or worried about something.

I asked my dad why he did it once and he said, "It's my way of telling you everything is going to be alright." Every time I was nervous before a swim meet or a dance recital, he used to take my hand and squeeze it, and I instantly felt better.

Henry squeezing my hand reminds me of home.

Reminds me that everything is going to be alright.

And the swirl of nervousness in my belly reminds me

They're really going to make me stand up in this roller coaster seat. At an *angle*.

I watch the technicians assist the people in the front first. Lots of shaky legs walk down the steps, hands gripping the railing like a lifeline. The park employees get closer and closer to Josh and Diana, and our morbid curiosity on what they look like overrides our terror at standing up and exiting our seats.

It's ultimately anticlimactic. Josh has some flesh-colored, patchy scruff on his jaw and glares at us as he walks off. Diana follows, wearing a high pony and a fashion fanny pack on her hip, her huge earrings swinging as she steps down the stairs.

"I think you're in the clear," I say to Henry. "Your ass won't be beat."

"I'm so relieved. If I don't die going down those steps, we're so making out," Henry says, lifting his arms as far as the harness would allow. I try to lift my arms too, and we try to reach for each other, but dramatically quit because of the harnesses.

It will be interesting to get off this ride. I hope our inevitable kiss isn't terrible. While I felt nothing when we first met, I've grown to have a raging crush on this man, cargo shorts and all.

"Are you still wet?" I ask.

"Absolutely for you, baby. Is it too soon to call you baby? How about schnookums?"

I giggle. "Baby is fine, baby."

He winks, and I laugh harder.

Finally, the employees are at our row.

"Okay, we're going to unlock these harnesses and help you step out. Ladies first," he says. He unlocks the bright green harness with a key and flips it up. I roll my shoulders and tilt my head from side to side. He offers me a hand, and I take it, standing up.

Don't look down, don't look down, I say to myself as I step onto the stairs. My knees almost give out as I move down three steps to give them room to get Henry out. They unlock his harness, and he steps out. He meets me a few steps down.

Please touch me, Henry. Usually, a guy would wrap his arm around my waist or shoulders, but Henry doesn't. We walk single-file down the ride and I finally look down.

There's news cameras with reporters and the fire department, as well as a huge crowd gathered, watching the stopped ride. I get closer to the ground, and relief washes over me. Seeing Erin's face in the crowd causes me to burst into tears...again. When I step off of the final stair onto the blacktop covering the ground, we're greeted by employees who shove a stack of cards at us.

Once we're through the exit, Henry drops to the ground and kisses the nasty blacktop like he's a solider returning to the US from the Second World War.

"Now I won't kiss you," I say. "Since your lips touched the ground."

Henry snaps his fingers with a swinging arm. "Damn, I knew it was too good to be true."

"Raegan!" Erin yells as she body-slams my chest and wraps her arms around me. We sway back and forth while Landon puts his hands on his hips, talking to Henry.

"I have to go to the bathroom," I announce and pull Erin by the elbow. It's been an hour and a half of being trapped on that ride, plus I need to discuss what happened with Henry.

My chest sinks as I leave Henry and Landon discussing. He's back to ignoring me.

No hug when we got to the bottom, no kiss. He kissed the *ground* instead of kissing me. I went from being completely uninterested to intrigued with him and excited about making out to freaking out that Henry might've only been flirting with me because we were trapped and he was bored.

I take care of business, and when I walk out, Erin is leaning against a wall with her arms crossed.

"What happened up there?" Erin asks.

I pump soap into my hands and lather them, running them under the cold water.

"I like him."

"Yes!" Erin cheers. "I love being right."

"No," I say. "I really, really like him."

"I told you. Maybe the roller coaster stopping was fate helping you out."

I rinse off my hands. Who knows how the date would've gone if we didn't have time away from our friends to talk and get to know each other? To flirt. To connect.

I've never felt this close to a man on the first date. Ever.

"This is horrible timing," I say.

"You could stay in San Francisco, you know. If you need a place to stay..."

"I'm not moving in with you," I say. Erin and Landon own a cute two-bedroom apartment in the Marina District, and I have no money to contribute. It's time to be sensible.

I'm about to say fuck it and figure out a way to stay.

"I'm not going to stay for a guy," I say, although I'm not sure. "And anyway, he was weird when we got off of the ride. I expected...something."

A kiss. A kiss was what I expected. He kissed the damn ground instead.

"You did just get off of a stuck roller coaster," Erin says as I follow her out of the bathroom. We walk past a kiosk selling merchandise, and I pull out the cards in my pockets. It's for drink coupons and front-of-the-line passes, and I separate them out. I hand Erin the ride passes.

"I'm done with rides today," I say.

"Oh, okay," Erin says. "What do you want to do instead?"

Henry's words leak into my memory. *If we ever get off this ride, we have to ditch Landon and Erin.*

"Eat cotton candy and people-watch," I say.

We find Henry and Landon talking by the exit for the Double Helix. My breath catches in my throat as I approach Henry. His hands are settled in his pockets, and his mouth bursts into a bright smile. Maybe I wasn't reading him wrong?

He offers his hand to me, and I take it. He squeezes it three times and looks at Erin and Landon. "I want to hang out with Raegan alone, if that's okay."

All the wondering is gone. He wants to run away with me.

Well, for the rest of the day, at least.

My own face breaks into a huge grin.

"Fine," Erin and Landon say together. Smugness covers their faces as they study our body language, our joined hands. Henry pulls me away from them, and I wave goodbye. He breaks into a run, and I follow him. We weave in and out of crowds, my hand in his. I feel like a kid, free of any adult worries or fear.

I'm just having the best time with a boy I like.

Once we're far enough away from them, he ducks between two carnival booths, pulling me with him. He backs me against a wall and stares at me. My breath quickens as his lips hover inches from mine. His hand drifts down to my waist, and he grips my hip before dipping his head to kiss me.

Heat prickles my cheeks and my neck as his lips touch mine, soft and firm, and then he pulls away before I can even register it. His eyes flit to mine, and I grab the back of his head and really crush our lips together.

Never in my life could I have predicted Henry's kisses.

The kiss sizzles as his tongue breaches my lips, lazily playing with mine. His hand plays with one of my pink curls as he brushes it over my shoulder. My body is overwhelmed with this kissing, his hands on me. His hand cradles the back of my head tenderly, and I want to be kissed like this for the rest of my life.

"This is so much fun," Henry says when he pulls away, gasping for breath.

"Then don't stop."

He smiles, and his lips are back on mine. Our heads move side to side, our movements in perfect sync. His fingertips on my skin trace paths of spark, and when he pulls me to him, I feel his broad chest. My hand weaves around his body to feel his strong back muscles. Being so close in height works to our advantage. No one is craning their neck, so we can just keep kissing.

His lips work their way down my jawline, finding a ticklish part near my ear. I snort-laugh, and his breath scorches my skin as he laughs at the noise I made.

I've never been kissed like this before. It's like Henry has no agenda, no end goal. It's innocent and fun. I moan as he kisses my neck.

"Oh, *gross*," we hear and turn to see the same kid from the water ride who teased Henry. Henry freezes, and I break away, wiping my mouth with my hand.

The kid has dried off considerably and holds a churro. My stomach growls at the proximity to delicious cinnamon and sugar.

"You said he wasn't your boyfriend," the kid says.

"He's not," I say.

"We're lovers," Henry yells at the kid, and he retreats. My face flames. After a kiss like that, all I can think about is Henry between my legs, thrusting into me. I brace myself against the booth before I stumble.

"Gross," the kid says again. Someone calls out "Tristan," and the kid pivots. He turns back and says, "Later, old people. Wear protection."

Henry rests his hands on his hips. "Where in the hell did he learn that?"

"He interrupted us," I say.

"How rude of him," Henry says, crossing his arms. "Whoever taught him about protection obviously didn't teach him manners."

I cross my arms. "Can we forgo the cotton candy? That kid made me want a churro."

"I think I just fell in love with you," Henry says, wrapping his arm around my shoulders. "Let's go get one and hope we never run into that weasel again."

I think I just fell in love with you vibrates through my skull. If any other date had said that to me, I would've found a reason to leave, asked my friend to call me with a fake emergency. With Henry, it doesn't scare me at all.

We leave our make-out cove in search of churros and walk toward the collection of walk-up ordering queues, full of people ordering and picking up food barely resembling nutrition.

My stomach rumbles, and I check my watch. Three-thirty. No wonder.

"Actually, churro later. I might get actual food. Well, the closest thing they have to food here."

"Smart," Henry says. "What looks good? Fake Mexican? Fake Chinese? A very real corn dog?"

"I can't remember the last time I had a corn dog. "Let's do it."

We walk to the island of a corn dog stand with a red-and-white tented roof. Two apathetic teenagers are working in it, barely cracking a smile at each new guest.

We wait in line, and I lean into him, my hand snaking around his waist. He kisses the green portion of my hair, and when it's our turn, we walk and order two hot-link corn dogs and two Diet Cokes with our free food coupons. We find the least stickiest table and doctor ours up. I prefer straight ketchup while he does a ketchup/mustard mixture, swirling it into an orange sauce in his cardboard boat.

Mustard used to be a dealbreaker. Not anymore. I will gladly kiss him again. I might gag if I smell mustard, but I won't care.

"Oh my God," Henry says, his mouth full of corn dog.

His eyes bug, his bite crowded in his cheek like he's a chipmunk. "This is delicious. Why don't I get these more often?"

I take a bite of mine. It's fresh and hot, the breading melting in my mouth and the spiciness of the sausage taking a second to kick in. Once it does, there is so much flavor, and my eyes roll back in pleasure.

There's so many opportunities here for sexual innuendos, but I make none. With Henry, I don't have to perform. I don't have to be something I'm not. This date with Henry is one of the biggest surprises of my time in San Francisco.

A time that is quickly coming to an end.

Waves of sadness roll over me as I look at him. I accepted this date since I expected it would go nowhere. Now I'm trying to figure out what we can do. A guy who doesn't do long distance. And now I'm leaving.

"You look sad," Henry asks. "Should we have gotten two corn dogs?"

"No," I say, wiping my hand on a napkin. I lick the remaining ketchup residue from my palm. "When I said I'm leaving San Francisco, I'm moving. Back to my hometown. In two days."

"Goldheart?" he asks.

I nod. *He remembered.* "My contract is up with my job, and it's time to determine my next steps. It's time to be an adult."

"You look like an adult to me." Henry wiggles his eyebrows, and I touch his forearm.

"No, I need to get serious," I say, repeating a conversation I had with my older sister. "I've had my fun. I got to live my dream of being in San Francisco. It's time to figure out my life. What I want to do. Who I want to be."

"I think you're pretty awesome just the way you are," Henry says.

"Thanks," I say. I don't feel awesome. I have barely five hundred dollars to my name, spotty work experience, and a wanderlust that has gotten me in trouble in the past. I'm twenty-seven, and I feel like I'm behind everyone my age.

Usually, I hide this under smiles, but I feel safe with Henry. "I'm running out of money. This was only supposed to be temporary, to get San Francisco out of my system. My parents will let me crash with them for a little bit, and my sister Annie said I can work at the winery with her while I figure everything out. What my next move is."

My breath catches as I wait for Henry to say something. I expect him to be angry that I agreed to this date when our relationship would go nowhere, that he'll suggest we end things now. His face shows me nothing, no disappointment, no sadness. His eyes grow determined as he crumples a napkin into a ball.

"Well, if you're leaving," he begins, "let's make this the best goddamn day we've ever had. Starting now. I need a delicious churro."

5

W e've turned into that annoying couple you see in public.

After we get churros, Henry rips off pieces and feeds them to me. At one point, my tongue grazes his thumb, and Henry waggles a finger at me.

"Naughty," Henry says. "However, feel free to lick me again. Anytime."

Not sure what possesses me, but I lick his ear, and he squirms with ticklishness and then he licks me back on my cheek.

If this isn't some weird mating ritual, I don't know what is.

This delicious treat is erasing all the drama of earlier— the stopped ride, the wave that nailed Henry, our teenage nemesis. It even makes me forget that I'm leaving.

My heart aches that this might be the only date I have with Henry.

A man I was *convinced* I wasn't going to like. A man I agreed to go on a date with because I was sure it wouldn't work out.

Henry travels the world, unattached, free to go where he pleases, and codes when he feels like it. His life sounds so romantic, but it also sounds like it has no room for me. Plus Henry is right; long-distance relationships aren't ideal. I was in one when I was a foreign exchange student in Paris, and it was so hard. It inevitably crumbled under the pressure, and then I had *a very* fun three months being single in my favorite city in the world. Henry broke up with someone before even attempting long distance. I assume he dated her for longer than a day. What hope did I have?

"What are you thinking about?" Henry asks, dipping his churro into a tub of chocolate sauce.

"How I'm leaving. How I'm having such a good time with you," I say.

"Yeah," he says, chewing, looking off into dead space. He turns back. "I was skeptical when Erin insisted I meet you. I told myself, 'there is no way this will work.' I mean, look at you."

"You could totally get it," I say, leaning in. He leans in too, and we give each other a whisper of a kiss. I taste the sugar and cinnamon on his lips, and I try to catalog this memory forever.

The opening guitar chords of "Party in the USA" by Miley Cyrus play over the intercoms, and Henry freezes like a prairie dog.

"This is my *jam*," he says, standing up. He offers a hand to me, and I slap mine with his. He leads me while dancing to the middle of a gazebo next to the eating area. Dancing in public can be nerve-wracking, but I don't care.

It's with Henry.

He grabs my hands and swings our arms together. He's mouthing every word, and I join him, singing to him, badly. When the chorus plays, we throw our hands up, we nod our heads, we swing our hips. Henry was hustling earlier. He is a *great* dancer.

"How come you don't dance with me in public like that, Josh?" a familiar voice says next to us. We turn and see Josh and Diana looking as happy as a couple in a waiting room at marriage counseling.

"Come on, Josh and Diana," Henry yells, ushering them over.

"Wait, how do you know our names?" Diana asks with crossed arms.

"High school," Henry lies and motions again. "Come on!"

Josh begrudgingly stands up after Diana basically rips his arm out. They join us as the chorus circles back and we mimic our hands in the air, the nodding, the hip shaking.

I look at Henry and smile as he takes me, dips me gracefully, and kisses me.

Am I in a musical? Am I in a romantic comedy?

He got Diana's Josh to dance. It's an amusement park miracle.

As the song winds down, I look at him. He's flailing, like he said he did while we were stuck. He doesn't care that it's not an "appropriate" way to dance. He just wants to.

That's how I live my life. I've never been someone who saves energy for the swim back, worried about drowning. I've always gone as hard as possible, giving my all, until I'm exhausted and spent.

Part of me wants to warn myself of the heartbreak to come if I throw myself into this. But I just don't care right now.

I grab his face for a kiss, languidly slow as the song flips to the next one. He lifts my hair from my neck and laces my strands between his fingers. I sigh against his lips. He pulls away and looks into my eyes.

"Do you want to get out of here?" Henry asks.

I nod, and he smiles, pressing his lips to mine again. His kisses send shots of fireworks throughout my body, and the thought of being alone with him, away from this amusement park, thrills me to my toes.

We high-five Josh and Diana before walking out of the gazebo, back to my purse and our trays of trash.

"Let me tell Erin I'm not coming home with them," I say. Henry nods once and takes the trays to throw them away.

I pull my phone out of my back pocket.

Me: Don't worry about us for a ride home.

The bubble for her typing pops up immediately.

Erin: I was right, wasn't I?!

Me: Yes.

Erin: Tell me everything at brunch tomorrow. Take detailed notes. Create a PowerPoint.

I laugh since PowerPoints are more my sister's thing, not mine.

Me: Will do.

Henry grabs my hand as we exit Thrill Mountain, thanking the employees at the entrance. I fish out the left-over vouchers we received for being stuck on the roller coaster and hand them to a confused woman by the exit.

"I'm parked way out there," Henry says, and I don't respond. Anything to spend more time with him.

"Did you keep a car while you were in Singapore?"

Henry nods. "I lent it to my friend, and I just got it back. My condo has parking included."

"I'm jealous. I'll have to get a car when I go home. I haven't driven in, like, a year."

We walk leisurely, our interconnected hands swinging

between us. Henry quietly asks, "Do you really have to leave?"

He turns his head and his eyes laser into me, but no matter how much I want to stay, no matter how much San Francisco feels like home to me, it's time to be serious. Going back to Goldheart will center me, help me figure out what to do with the rest of my life. So when I meet a man like Henry in the future, I can give my whole heart. The timing will be better. *I* will be better.

It just sucks that we found each other now.

"It's time to go home," I say.

"I understand that," Henry says. "The traveling was fun for a while. Now, I don't know. I like the idea of staying put for a while. But I might take off again. Who knows."

We find his car, a modest white sedan, and he opens my car door. I can't remember the last time a guy did that for me. When he sits down in the driver seat, he syncs up his phone to the stereo and turns on the car.

"Just between you and me, I'm relieved to be out of that park."

"Oh, me too. It's so not my thing."

"Me either. You know this, but Erin can be persuasive."

"Yeah," I say. "She wants details of what happens tonight."

"Of course she does," Henry says. "Let's give them something to talk about."

"Perfect," I say. His smile simmers into a hungry gaze, and I bite my lip.

Oh, he's totally getting laid tonight.

He pulls out of the parking lot of Thrill Mountain, and my excitement mounts.

I'm surprised with how light traffic is going back into the city. We arrive at his condo building in Potrero Hill, and we pull into an underground parking garage to a numbered spot. It's the equivalent of Henry flashing several hundred dollar bills, since nothing is a flex in San Francisco like having parking for a car.

I would kill to live in a building like Henry's. Sleek and modern, it seems to fit Henry's personality, and I cannot wait to see the inside. We walk up two flights of stairs to his unit. When he unlocks his door, I beeline to the window. His condo feels like a well-kept secret that overlooks a courtyard with benches and trees.

His condo is a studio, sparse and bare. Nothing hangs on the walls, and the only furniture is a yellow couch, a queen-sized bed and a glass coffee table. The only clutter is his wallet and keys on the kitchen counter. There's a small dog crate in the corner.

"Do you have a dog?" I ask.

"Well, kinda," he says. "I inherited a French bulldog from an old roommate before I lived with Landon. That dog has been living with my parents for the last year, and I think it's my mom's dog now."

I giggle, and he wraps his arms tentatively around my waist.

"So, what do you want to do?" Henry asks. "I have wine, and I think I have some cheese. There's year-old M&M's in my pantry..."

"Wine is great," I say. Usually, I don't get nervous when I go home with a man after a date, but this feels important since this probably will be the only time with Henry. I cross my arms and pace around the studio. If I sit down, the weight of the day and the ill-timing of this meeting might crush me.

He hands me a stemless glass of red wine, and I sip. Wow.

"This is really good," I say. I hold it up and examine it.

"Thanks, it's our old favorite," Henry says. I give him a confused look, and he says, "Trader Joe's."

"Our favorite," I say.

Henry sits down on his couch and pats the seat next to him. He rests his arm along the couch's back and I sit against his arm. His fingers play with my shirt's sleeve. My heart pounds as I look at him. How could I not be attracted to him from the very first moment? My mind is telling me to be reasonable and reminds me that I'm leaving, but my vagina is telling me to think about consequences later.

My decision is made for me when Henry leans in and kisses me, testing the waters. Our lips and tongues and breaths intertwine, and the way his hands rest tentatively on my skin makes me feel that there are no expectations tonight.

But I want to have sex with Henry.

I want to have sex with Henry very, very badly.

So I pull at the bottom of his shirt, and he stops my hand.

"I didn't invite you back here tonight to sleep with you. I hope you know that."

"Shut up and take my clothes off," I say.

"Yes, ma'am," he says, lifting my shirt over my head.

6

"You too," I say.

He grabs the neck off his shirt and pulls it off like only hot men do.

Holy shit. I did *not* know that Henry looked like that under his clothes. His pecs are chiseled, his abs have abs. I can't help but run my fingers down the ridges of his muscles. He has the most perfect nipples I'm ever seen.

"Wow," I say. "You look great with your shirt off."

"You do too, baby," he says, taking my mouth with his. The apex between my legs tightens as he pulls me onto his lap. I feel his hard length against me, and I grind against him. If I could swallow him whole, I would. Without warning, he stands up, and my legs wrap around his waist. He throws me on the bed and I bounce, so turned on I can't see straight.

Our kisses increase in urgency, feverish and unrelenting, his lips traveling down my throat to my cleavage. My skin ignites, and his palms on me, in between my legs, make me squeal. He tugs off my pants to reveal my matching panties, and his lips are on my belly, traveling down. Thank God, all my comfortable, but ugly underwear is dirty.

He spreads my knees apart and I'm panting with anticipation. Gone is the tentative man, Henry steams ahead, with a fire in his eyes.

"I feel like one lucky man. You are exquisite," he says as he hooks his thumbs under my underwear and yanks them down. I'm sure he can feel how soaked my panties were as he rolls them in his hand and tosses them to the side.

He lowers his lips to my clit and licks it once, and I cry out. "Yes," I plead through breathlessness.

"You like that?" he asks.

"Very much." He does it again, dragging his tongue achingly slow against it and flicks it as I arch my back, wanting him to be closer.

"You even taste exquisite," he says as he gets to work. He takes my clit and sucks, driving me over the edge. All that matters is his mouth on me, his fingers stroking the soft spot within me, how my orgasm is building, about to erupt at any moment. He flicks his tongue again against my clit, persistent and skilled.

Henry keeps surprising me.

I come unraveled, my pussy pulsating around his fingers. The roll of the wave finishes, and I lay there frozen.

His thoughtfulness, his attention to detail just gave me the best, strongest orgasm of my life.

"You are a goddamn expert," I say, dropping my forearm over my eyes.

He kisses me, and I taste myself on his lips. "I liked hearing you moan because of me," he says.

Two words...husband material.

I shake that thought loose because all I want is his cock inside of me.

"Do you have anything?" I ask.

"I think so," he says. He rolls over and opens a drawer under his bed. He pulls out a foil wrapper. "These are fresh, I promise. Landon gifted them to me."

"Did you think something was going to happen?" I ask, kissing his neck, touching his abs, running my hands over his chest.

"No, but I hoped so," he says as he stands up to drop his pants. "I like to be prepared."

His ass is so round, I reach forward and bite a cheek. He freezes.

Oh no. Why did you have to bite him, you weirdo?

"Are you going to bite the other cheek? Even it out?"

I laugh as I bite his other cheek, reaching around to cup his balls, causing him to gasp as he rolls the condom on.

"Come here, you," he says as he drags me across the bed by my ankles.

With some finesse, I'm now on top, straddling his muscular thighs, staring at him. His beautiful penis is smooth and hard in my hand.

"I need to be inside of you," he says as he grips my hips. "Ride me like a roller coaster."

I laugh and kiss him, his hands palming my breasts as I position him at my entrance.

When I sink down on him, we both exhale and he grips my ass.

"Holy shit," he says as he sits up.

The way he looks at me—damn. He pulls a bra strap off of my shoulders and kisses across my chest, and I roll into him, his cock filling me.

I ride him slowly at first, and the cold air puckers my nipples when he unhooks my bra and flings it onto his hardwood floor. He takes one of my breasts into his mouth, sucking my nipple, and I cry out as I moan into his hair. He anchors his arm under my ass and flips me onto my back, a move that shoots pleasure straight to my core, launching me to a new stratosphere of desire. Is it possible to reach a whole new level of orgasms?

He takes one of my ankles onto his shoulder, going deeper, making me gasp.

"Raegan," he says, as he kisses me and moans against my lips.

When he pulls away, his eyes lock with mine, and it hits me.

I just fit with this man. His gaze seeps into my soul, sees me for who I am. His thrusts speed up, my eyes roll into the back of my head, but I try to remember everything. How he kisses me, how his hands feel on me.

It's so good, but I know this is not forever. It can't be.

His breath quickens as he grows bigger in me, and when he finishes, he grunts from deep within.

He collapses on me, and I kiss his shoulder, dragging my fingernails up and down his back. When he lifts his head, he kisses me deeply, and I can't help it. A single tear rolls down my cheek.

THE NEXT MORNING, I wake up in Henry's arms. I check my watch, and my eyes bug out. When I stand up, Henry's basketball shorts fall off my hips.

My farewell brunch is in ten minutes, and I'm at least fifteen minutes away.

All I want is to stay in bed with Henry all day.

"Henry," I say urgently. He startles and jerks, his eyes opening like a newborn kitten's.

"Is something on fire?" he asks.

"I have brunch with my friends in like…eight minutes." I step into my jeans and hook my bra. I pull my shirt on, and he's rubbing his eyes. He stands up and wobbles.

God, he's so cute.

"I have to go. I don't know where my phone is. I have to order an Uber," I say.

"I'll drive you."

"You don't have to."

"I want to," he says, rubbing his hair.

"Thank you," I say, kissing him although his eyes are half-closed.

I could cancel on my friends. I could spend one more day with him.

No, brunch is sacred.

But he's so *cute.*

He steps into some slides and grabs his keys, and I find my phone stashed in my tiny backpack I wore to Thrill Mountain. We barely have time to talk about how this might be the last time we see each other, how last night was beyond my wildest dreams and my heart aches. We just focus on the task at hand, walking downstairs and climbing into his car to drive to Home Plate for brunch.

"Are you awake?" I ask.

"I will need about two gallons of coffee," he says, backing out of his parking spot after checking all his blind spots. "It was worth it, though. I can probably get there, but be my navigator, just in case."

"Definitely," I say. I pull up the directions on my phone, and we make lefts and rights.

We're stopped on 9ᵗʰ, waiting for a stoplight to change to cross Market, when he turns toward me and takes my hand up to his lips to kiss it. My throat grows thick in sorrow.

It kills me I met him two days before I'm leaving San Francisco. That a random, otherwise horrible day when I got stuck on a roller coaster could've been the worst day ever, but it turned out to be the best.

"How long are you staying in San Francisco?" I ask, my heart already missing him.

"I don't know," he says as the light turns green. "I have a meeting with a tech company here about a contract for coding some software. But if I get another project, I might take off. Who knows."

"Maybe I can come visit you," I say. "Before you leave."

"I don't know if that's a good idea," he says. He sniffles, and I see some glassiness to his light eyes. His lips curve downward, and his eyes blink.

My heart sinks. "Why not?"

"It'll be too hard. If I see you again, it will be even harder to accept...well...you know."

I know exactly what he means. A small part of me imagined him coming over tonight, eating pizza in between boxes, having sex on my sleeping bag since I sold my bed last week so all my stuff would fit in my sister's car. Knowing I have minutes before I have to say goodbye to him makes me want to bawl.

I've had one-night stands, but this feels more than that —more important, more pivotal. I've never had so much fun with someone, felt so safe, felt so cared for. This is what I was looking for on all those dating apps, when I went on the single cruises around the bay. It's what Erin found on an airplane. It's what Cassie found in an elevator.

My story does not end like theirs. My story with Henry ends today.

We reach Home Plate way too soon. We pull into the Wells Fargo parking lot adjacent to the restaurant, and

Henry finds an angled spot to pull into. I check my watch. I'm late by ten minutes, but I don't care. I hug Henry.

I can't help it, I start to cry.

"It's okay," he soothes, and that just makes me cry harder. It's not okay. It's cruel and stupid and makes me wish things were different. We pull away from each other and kiss, and he kisses the tears away from my eyes. The rims of his eyes are red too as he looks at me.

"It was so nice to meet you," he says, pushing my hair away from my face.

"It feels more important than that," I say, hugging him.

"I know." His voice cracks, and it makes my tears slip faster.

We kiss one more time. We hold each other for seconds or years, I don't know, and I know one thing for sure.

I don't want to say goodbye.

"Come in," I say. "The girls won't mind. It'll be a little awkward but..."

"I can't," he says into my hair, kissing where his words went. "It'll be too hard."

"I understand," I say, although my voice quivers. When we pull away, his hand still rests on my arm.

"I just wish..." he says. "I just wish things were different."

"Me too."

He kisses me one more time. "Goodbye."

"Bye," I say. I walk down the parking lot aisle, but I look back to where he's parked. His car does not move, does not turn on. Every two steps, I look back to see his figure in the car, just sitting in the driver's seat.

It makes me want to sob.

7

"Oh my God, what happened to you?" Cassie asks, as I approach the table.

"You're wearing the same outfit as yesterday," Erin says, looking me up and down. An evil smirk crosses her lips. "Were you with Henry?"

I say nothing as I plop down in the empty chair at the table.

It's just Cassie and Erin today for brunch. Our other friend, Sarah, had a family function she couldn't get out of. She and I grabbed dinner earlier in the week, and she got me beautiful flowers that I gifted to my roommate since I wouldn't be able to enjoy them much longer.

"Oh, right, that was supposed to happen yesterday. It went well, I guess?" Cassie asks.

I get a glimpse of the giant diamond ring on Cassie's finger. I didn't feel an ounce of jealousy when I helped with the engagement surprise, but after what happened with Henry...

I can barely hear the ladies over my sobbing.

"Oh no," I hear Cassie say. "What happened?"

"I got stuck on a roller coaster. I wasn't interested in Henry, and then he became really cute and then we danced to 'Party in the USA' in the middle of the food court..."

"That *is* Henry's jam," Erin says.

"So, you did just come from Henry's condo?" Cassie asks. The server came and took our orders, bottomless mimosas all around. I look around Home Plate, our brunch spot for countless weekends. It didn't matter how dire my finances became, I always scrounged up money for a brunch with Erin, Cassie, and Sarah. I'm sad Sarah couldn't make it today.

I start crying again.

"You are a mess today. More than usual," Erin says.

"I'm going to miss San Francisco. And you guys. And Henry..." My face crinkles like a paper ball, and I'm bawling again. A toddler at the next table stops his temper tantrum and looks at me, alarmed.

"What happened with Henry?" Erin asks.

"I like him. I really like him." I do not add that what I feel is a strong like on the bullet train to love. If I had two more weeks, I would say "I love you" and move in if he asked me. I would accept a proposal after two months. I could even go down to six weeks.

"Did you sleep with him?" Cassie asks.

I nod. I drop my forehead to the table with too much force, and the bang makes me yelp in pain.

"Don't give yourself a concussion," Erin says.

I lift my head. "Erin, this is all your fault."

She throws her hands up. "You're welcome for the sex last night. It was good, wasn't it?"

"So good." I sob again.

"I did not expect this," Cassie says. "Goddammit, I owe you dinner."

"What?"

Erin looks a tiny bit smug. "Cassie didn't think you would hit it off, and I was convinced you would. So, I win."

"What do I do now?" I ask. "I can't live a normal life after him. He's ruined me."

"He doesn't want to keep talking?" Erin asks.

I shake my head. "We just said goodbye in the Wells Fargo parking lot."

"That fucker," Erin says. She picks up her phone, but I place my hand on it.

"Don't," I say, sniffling and wiping my nose on my napkin. "I don't think he and I should keep talking either."

The server brings the first round. The champagne helps.

"I'm so sorry, Raegan," Erin says. "I just knew you two would hit it off, and that's why I pushed so hard. I thought at the very least he would stay in San Francisco, and maybe you could commute to see each other if it worked out. He's just been out of town for so long, and I thought..."

"It's okay, Erin. I'm glad I met him. That way I know what I won't settle for. Henry is my new gold standard."

I hoped saying that out loud would alleviate the deep ache in my chest. My heart feels like it's been ripped in two. I can forget Henry. This will pass. I knew him for less than twenty-four hours. Maybe the intensity I feel is *because* it was so short and it had an ending.

"That's the spirit," Erin looks down. "I'm really sorry. Maybe it would have been better if you didn't know."

"You have nothing to be sorry about," I say. My tears dry, and certainty flows over me. I feel clear about going back to my hometown when I felt so unsure about it just yesterday. I can recover from San Francisco there. I can recover from Henry there.

"We'll come visit you in Goldheart," Cassie says. "We could go to Lake Tahoe for a girls' weekend."

"That sounds fun," I say.

"Maybe we'll meet another Zoey," Erin says.

"I wish," Cassie replies.

They always talk about the friend's bachelorette party they went to and how much fun it was and how they want to go back to that club. They still talk to a woman they met in the bathroom there randomly, even attended her wedding where they caught the officiant with a woman in the supply closet who had a streak of pink in her hair.

"I wish I met you the first day I moved to San Francisco," I say, holding out my hands. They take my hands in theirs, their soft smiles confirmation they feel the same. "You have been great friends to me and have made my time in San Francisco so special."

"You leave your heart in San Francisco. It's cheesy as hell, but they're totally right, whoever 'they' are. I was so excited to come to the city today because I miss it," Cassie says. "But you're always welcome back. You can sleep on my couch whenever you want."

Cassie just moved with her fiancé to San Rafael in Marin County. Their townhome is so cute and so them. I wish I would be closer. I won't after Monday.

"You can stay on my couch too. And you're coming back for my wedding in a few months," Erin says.

"There's that," I say. "Is Henry going to be there?"

Erin nods. "He's the best man."

I breathe in and out. "It will be good to see him. Hopefully my heart won't feel like this then."

"Hopefully not," Cassie says. "But what if it does?"

"I have to accept that we're victims of bad timing," I say, playing with my napkin. Maybe if I keep saying things like this, I will start believing it's true. "Who knows? Maybe I'll meet a cement mixer technician and forget completely about Henry."

"I still feel so bad," Erin says.

"You should feel bad about the roller coaster. However, I'm glad I met Henry."

Our memories from yesterday roll into my mind. Making fun of Josh and Diana on the ride, then dancing with them in the gazebo. The way his hand felt in mine and how the feelings intensified every time he touched me. The corn dogs and the churros. The way he looked into my soul while we made love.

My phone buzzes, and my heart lunges. Everything sinks when I see who messaged me. My sister Annie.

Annie: Pick you up tomorrow at noon?

Me: Yes. See you then.

"Is that Henry?" Erin asks.

I shake my head, dropping my phone back into my purse. "Sister."

"I can't believe it. Time goes by so fast."

"I can't believe it, either. God, so much has changed. I got engaged. You got engaged and moved and left me..." Erin says to Cassie.

"We met Raegan," Cassie says. "This feels like so much change."

"It is," I say. "But it's good though. You met the love of your life, and I got to live in San Francisco. It's time to go home and get my head on straight."

"Well, the minute you feel antsy or miss SF, you come and visit us," Erin says. "Promise?"

"Absolutely," I say. "We need to do a toast."

We raise our champagne flutes to one another.

"To being stuck in love," I say.

Cassie and Erin coo at my toast, and we clink glasses. The champagne gives me unbridled optimism.

Everything will be okay.

I will figure everything out.

I will recover from Henry, and one day, I won't feel like my heart is so heavy that my chest is sinking through my butt.

Unfortunately, all great adventures come to an end.

THE NEXT DAY, my sister arrives forty-five minutes early.

"I didn't expect traffic to be that light for a Monday," she says when I let her in. "Oooh, I love your hair! Very siren-esque."

"Thanks," I say. Sometimes, curling my hair calms me so my hair is extra fluffy today. The last time I saw my sister, my hair was completely green.

"Are you sad?" Annie asks, putting her hand on my shoulder. I nod, and she pulls me in for a hug. I cry softly into the cotton of her shirt, and she rubs my back like she's done a million times before.

Annie is seven years older than me and technically my half-sister, but we're incredibly close, and the upside of moving home is I'll get to see her every day. She has always encouraged me, never doubted me, never told me what I want to do is stupid. However, when I called her to tell her that I was running out of money and men to date in San Francisco, she was the one to suggest I come home.

"Goldheart will ground you," she said, and I agreed with her at first. Now, I'm not so sure.

Annie points to my stuff in the corner. "Is this it?"

I nod. My entire life in San Francisco crowds one corner

by the couch. Four boxes, multiple totes loaded with my random junk, and two pieces of luggage. It doesn't look like much or even a fair representation of what this city means to me. It takes three trips to my sister's Jeep to load everything in. Somehow, I have less stuff than what I started with, since I sold all my big furniture and other items I didn't need any more when my finances dwindled considerably.

I give my key to my roommate and hug her goodbye. When we leave, I look up at my building, a crumbling Victorian fourplex, to the top floor where I lived. I remember the laughs, the bad dates, the late nights, and how I cried over Henry last night in my sleeping bag so loud, my roommate checked on me to see if I was okay. My throat is thick, and my head still hurts from all the crying.

Coming here did not satisfy my wonder about the city. It made it worse.

Suddenly, leaving feels like cutting off an arm.

"You can always come back to visit. You have friends who live here. You can hop on the BART and come in whenever you want," Annie suggests.

"It won't be the same," I say as we pull away. Tears fall down my cheeks as we drive down away from my street, from my life in San Francisco. When Annie merges onto Highway 80 to head home, she looks at me and sees the tears still flowing down my cheeks.

"I know how much you loved it there. At least you got to live there, even if it was only for a little while."

It wasn't enough, I think, watching the billboards and buildings pass.

"You're really quiet. You're not usually this quiet," Annie says.

"I know. I met a guy," I say. I feel fresh out of crying, but the tears hang out behind my eyes, ready to come out if I say one more word about him.

"When?"

"Saturday," I say.

"Wow, bad timing," Annie says.

"Totally," I say, wiping my nose with my hand.

"Do you want to tell me about him?" she asks.

"Not right now," I say. Time to change the subject. "So, what's going on with Jason?"

Annie focuses on the road without a word. Annie has secretly been seeing her boss's son at the winery for over a year and is head over heels in love with him. I try to be supportive, but my sister could do so much better than Jason Banning.

"I don't know," Annie says. "I want us to tell his dad, but Jason doesn't want to. Doesn't think it's the right time because his parents' wedding anniversary is coming up and they're planning this huge party. I don't know. I'm tired of being hidden, you know?"

I grab my sister's hand and squeeze it three times, remembering how Henry holding mine gave me so much comfort. Telling her she can do better than Jason does nothing. My father has been telling me since the beginning to settle down, stop moving around, to be sensible.

It never worked. Only Annie was able to talk me into it.

"Thank you for getting me," I say as we leave the city behind. My heart feels worse.

"Of course. I can't wait to have my baby sister home," Annie says.

I smile at her, but inside, I wonder how long I can stay there before I want to get out.

8

Goldheart is how I left it, but the buildings look smaller, the streets narrower. The first weekend back, we walk down Main Street, and Annie pops in to say hello to the owners of various shops, including Mr. Lathrop who owns the bookstore in town and just lost his wife.

Annie walks out with a wave behind her. I squirm in my skin. "You know everyone," I say, crossing one arm across from me. A woman I do not know stares at me from across the street. I'm not sure if she's a tourist or resident. Goldheart usually gets busy in the summer, if people are at the lake nearby or here for the day to get that small-town charm or shop at the small businesses. Goldheart has been vigilant on keeping chain stores and restaurants out, so you have to go the next town over if you want Starbucks.

When the conversation becomes quiet, I think about Henry. I wonder what he's doing, what new exotic location he might be heading off to. If I think too long, I obsess over our day and night together, how perfect it was, and I listen to Miley Cyrus and cry.

"How are you feeling?" Annie asks, touching my shoulder as we walk.

I shrug one shoulder.

A couple walk by and hold up a hand. "Hi, Annie. Is this your sister from the city?"

I smile closed-mouthed as Annie wraps an arm around me. "Yes, this is Raegan. She's back. For now."

"How long did you live there?" he asks.

I swallow and say, "Sixteen months."

"Ah," the woman says. "I don't know how anyone could live there. The homeless problem and how dirty it is. It's fun to go into the city for a baseball game, but other than that, I avoid it as much as possible. I enjoy it here much more."

I'm not sure how to respond. She has valid points about the state of the city, but it's obvious it hasn't crept into her soul like it has mine.

I just want to go back.

"That's your opinion, Miriam," Annie says sweetly. I know inside her head she's cursing her out. My sister would never say it out loud, though. "Raegan loves it there."

"Someone has to live there," she says. "Well, we won't take up too much more of your time. Say hi to your father for us. Come on, Leland."

Her husband trails her as they pass us. I snarl, and Annie giggles at me. I have to get used to small-town gossip again.

Annie says. "Have you heard from Henry?"

I shake my head. It's been almost a week, and I'm not sure what I expected from him. He's not on social media, so it saves me from watching his content for clues. We didn't exchange numbers, deliberately. Is he as broken up as me about our time together? What is he doing? Is he seeing another woman already? I'm not sure at this point if knowing or not knowing is beneficial.

"I just don't know if it bothers him as much as it bothers me."

"I'm sure he's broken up over you. You're too awesome for a guy to get over you so easily." She kisses my head, and we keep walking.

"What's going on with Jason? He was in quite the hurry yesterday."

Jason came over last night. When I opened the door, he stepped back, shocked that someone knew he was visiting Annie. I let him in, and he was as jumpy as the drug addicts I used to pass on Market. Annie and Jason disappeared into her room, and then he left forty-five minutes later, like he was on a timer.

Annie says nothing as we reach the end of the main drag and see a red barn in the distance. Staying with Annie, I've noticed some things. She constantly checks her phone. Getting a text from Jason is like a hit of crack. The highs are so high and the lows are low. I would've flipped out on him by now, but my sister has been way too nice. "You look like you need a drink."

"Definitely," I say. I vaguely remember this building, and I go through my memories and knowledge of the town. "Wait, is that new?"

"It's always been there. The Finches spruced it up, and now their brewhouse is there," Annie says. The Woody Finch Brewery has been a fixture in Goldheart for the last three years, but it seems like the Finch family has really upped their game recently.

"Are all the kids still there?" I ask, even though the Finch siblings are all older than me by at least five years.

"Yes. Emily, Cameron, and Reid all stayed in town, but Jackson just moved home."

"Wow, I remember this place being rundown and almost condemned," I say as Annie leads me onto the gravel driveway, past picnic benches filled with families and through the open barn doors.

It is *packed*. The Finches must be doing well.

"There's a long high table over there," Annie says. "Grab us a spot. What do you want?"

"A cider, if they have one," I say.

"Coming right up," Annie says, walking to the bar. Cameron's working behind it today. I would notice him anywhere. Six-five, he has a reputation of sleeping with eighty percent of the single, available women in town and ninety percent of the tourists. To the best of my knowledge, he has never hooked up with Annie, and I hope it stays that way.

Sitting alone, next to other couples chatting and families enjoying each other's company, I wonder if I could ever fit in here. I haven't lived here more than a few months on summer break from college, and since then, I've barely come home except for a day or two here and there for visits or holidays.

My phone buzzes, and I look up. Annie is chatting with Cameron, and he has a big smile on his face as he talks to her. I shoot daggers at him so he will at least instinctively know not to mess with my sister.

Erin: How are you? We miss you.

I want to cry.

Me: Me too.

Erin: How does it feel to be back?

Me: Weird. I'll have to get used to it. I like being with my sister, though.

Erin: My couch is always open.

Me: I'll keep that in mind.

Annie rejoins me with my cider in a pint glass and a golden, cloudy beer in a snifter for her.

"What do we cheers to?" Annie asks.

I remember the last cheer with my friends, and I lift my glass.

"To being from here," I say.

"Don't sound so excited," Annie says as our glasses touch.

The quiet music playing over the brewery switches to "Party in the USA," and I set my cider down.

"Are you okay?" Annie asks me before I realize what is happening. I'm slumped over the table, sobbing.

I lift my head. "No. I'm not."

"What is it?"

It's everything. How one day with Henry made me question everything. How that city wormed its way into my soul and I can't be happy living anywhere else. How being home this last week has felt like my soul is dying.

It becomes clear to me what I have to do. Miley singing takes me right back to how I felt dancing with Henry at Thrill Mountain. How I've never felt so comfortable, so alive. How my future has to be in San Francisco, not here in Goldheart. How my future is with Henry.

My tears dry, and everything becomes so clear. "I think I have to go."

Annie follows me out of the brewery. "Where are you going?"

"I think I have to go back to San Francisco," I say. "I have to."

I walk in the direction of Annie's car, parked in a public parking spot behind Town Square.

If I get an Uber to the El Centro BART station, I can take the BART to the 24th St. Mission...

"You're just adjusting. Let's go home. You're tired," Annie says, following me.

"I'm not," I say.

"This is crazy," Annie says. "Raegan, I...Wait. Who's that?"

I turn around to see Henry searching the street, holding a collection of green, blue, and pink flowers. His face bursts into a smile when he sees me, and I break into a run.

Somehow, I end up in his arms like a needy koala.

"Hi," he says into my hair, his hand under my butt.

"Hi," I say, smiling so hard it hurts. "What are you doing here?"

"I came here to find you," Henry says. "I'm going to put you down before I drop you."

"Okay," I say as he sets me down.

He's here. I'm not hallucinating.

"Let's sit down," he says, leading me by hand to a bench where the bus picks up. He hands me the flowers, and I smell them.

He takes one of my hands in his. "Our date together was so special. I kept wondering why Erin set up a date on your last weekend in San Francisco, and now I know why. She saw something in us that we couldn't see. I need you in my life, Raegan. I would love to be friends, but..." Henry pauses. "I'm not sure I can only be friends with you. The sex was just too good."

I laugh and then, I breathe in to avoid any more tears.

He's here. For me.

"What are you saying?" I ask.

"Be with me," he says. "Even if we're long distance for a little bit."

He hugs me, and his strong arms around me, the way he smells, how he kisses my hair makes me feel like I've found my person.

Henry is the one I've been looking for.

He pulls away from me with rosy cheeks.

"Is that your sister?" Henry points to Annie, who is watching us with crossed arms. I nod.

Henry walks over to Annie, and I can't hear what he's saying. I'm sure Annie is giving her usual spiel, that she owns a shovel and no one would find his body if he hurts me.

She hugs him, and they walk back to me. Henry intertwines his fingers with mine and warmth flows through my body.

"Get out of here," Annie says with a hand wave.

"You don't mind?"

"No," Annie says. "One of the Finch siblings is bound to keep me company and finish your drink."

"Not Cameron," I say with a finger point.

"Whatever, Mom," Annie says. "Cameron wouldn't be interested in me anyway."

What a crock of shit. My sister is tall and beautiful, and she has a vagina. Cameron would definitely be interested, even if he says he isn't.

Henry and I walk out the brewery and down the gravel road. He turns next to a meadow, the sun setting behind a hill. It castes a golden hue over the grass and makes his eyes squint.

He's so cute.

"So, how is this going to work?" I ask.

"I'm not leaving San Francisco until we figure out if this can work or not," Henry says. "No more traveling. I know you need to figure out some stuff here, and I'll be busy in the city. Still, I want to see you on every one of your days off. We can trade off who visits whom. I want to talk to you every night. We can make this work until we know for sure. I just need to know."

"Erin told me I could stay on her couch so I can be back in San Francisco," I say. He lights up and takes my face in his hands, kissing me.

I feel like I'm in a Hallmark movie.

"Come back to me," he says. I want to melt into a puddle.

San Francisco. A place I thought was only temporary. Thinking about living there, really living there, makes me giddy. It's the same feeling I had on the plane to France for my study abroad, how I felt crossing the borders into a dozen new countries. Doing what I want to do, life feeling so right I know it in my bones.

"San Francisco," I say, bringing my hands to my heart.

Henry loops his arms around my middle. "Just watch—you'll be living with me within a week."

"At least six weeks," I say and kiss him. Linking my arms around his neck, I pull him closer. It's a kiss of hope and promise.

"I'm so glad I met you," Henry says.

"I'm so glad I met you too," I reply, nuzzling into the crook of his neck.

"I have one stipulation for our relationship."

"What's that?" I ask, kissing his neck. We need to find somewhere private, pronto.

He leans down so his lips are next to the shell of my ear. "No more roller coasters."

"Done," I say.

He dips me like he did at the park and kisses me, and I can't believe this is happening to me.

How funny life is. I should never plan anything because

EPILOGUE

"Wow," Annie says as Henry and I walk into the brewery, ready to win.

We're wearing matching shirts with "Team We Can't Stop" written across them, along with matching sweat headbands and wristbands in obnoxious yellow. There might only be five pairs of people showing up to trivia tonight, but we plan to crush every last one of them. We've been honing our skills at several bar trivia nights across the city, so we're unstoppable.

"Are you intimidated?" Henry asks, posturing with open arms to my sister. My sister laughs as Henry leans over her table and whispers, "I can feel you're intimidated."

"Baby, keep that fire for trivia," I say. "Is there a trophy? I feel like there should be a trophy."

"Are they always like this?" Emily Finch asks. Emily's family owns Woody Finch Brewery, and she's agreed to be my sister's partner for trivia after Jason canceled.

"Unfortunately," Annie says.

Henry dips me in a kiss, and then we high-five.

We've become that annoying couple. In three short

months, Henry has become my best friend who I sleep with almost every day. We finish each other's sentences, we spend all our free time together, and he makes me feel like I can conquer the world. He came home for Thanksgiving with me and I met his family at Christmas.

I only made it a week in Goldheart before Henry showed up to move me home.

Back to San Francisco.

I always lived my life with a heart wide open, and everything in me told me I had to do this.

The first week back in the city, I was offered a position at an international school because I'm fluent in French. I don't know why I didn't pursue that all along. Teaching young children a language I love, in a city I love, being with the man I love is a dream come true.

After six weeks of sleeping on Erin and Landon's couch, Henry came over one day with a pizza. When I opened it, I saw a flat box in the corner. My heart stopped. When I opened the box, I found a key.

"I love you, Raegan. And I can't stand being away from you one more night," he said. "Move in with me."

A tear slipped down my cheek as I accepted, kissing him until our lips grew numb. A key was wonderful, and it was crazy, but six weeks was long enough for me to know.

Henry is who I want to marry, who I want to grow old with. Some people need years, some people need months. All I needed was forty-two days. That heart-drop feeling when it was a key instead of a ring signaled to me that I had found him. I was done searching.

Now he's back in Goldheart with me for his first official visit. He met my parents. We walked down Main Street like we've been together for years. Mrs. Epstein, the librarian who I've known since I was a baby, pulled me aside afterward and told me he was perfect for me.

I couldn't agree more.

"Is your brother ready for this?" Annie asks Emily.

Emily shrugs. "We'll see. We've been trying to do more events like this with varied results. Hopefully Dan can see we're making an effort."

I look around and see four other couples waiting at tables for trivia to start. Cameron Finch, Emily's brother, walks out with pads of paper and tiny pencils, and hands them out to couples participating. Cameron's gaze falls on Henry, and they give each other a quick nod.

"Do you know Cameron?" I ask.

"Oh yeah," Henry says with a nervous giggle. I look at Cameron and back at Henry. Henry can't look me in the eye.

Something is up.

"Baby, you're acting shifty," I say.

"What are you talking about?" Henry asks, with a "I don't know" gesture.

Cameron takes a corner with a stool and the microphone. He speaks into it quietly.

"Hello everyone. Welcome to the first Woody Finch Trivia Night. I'm your host, Cam."

"Go, Cam!" Annie yells with a whoop. I'm not sure why Annie is so nice to him. They've always been friendly, but not *too* friendly, with one another. Cameron and Emily's brother Reid has been Annie's best friend since childhood, and I kinda wish they would get together. However, my sister looks at Cameron in a way I'm not completely comfortable with.

"Thanks, Annie," Cameron says into the microphone. He pulls the first card up.

"Which *Final Destination* film starts with a premonition

of a roller coaster accident?" Cameron reads off. "Is it a. #1, b., #2, or c., #3?"

I write down a "c" on our sheet.

"I knew that one too, by the way," Henry says, his hand on my thigh. "I know how much you *love Final Destination.*"

"You're funny," I say.

"You love me," he says, kissing me on my cheek. Even after our short three months, the honeymoon phase is strong and he still gives me butterflies.

"Okay," Cameron says, pulling up the next card. "Where is the tallest roller coaster in the world? Is it a. Japan, b. New Jersey, or c. Canada?"

Why is the trivia all about roller coasters?

I look at Henry, and he shakes his head. He's usually more help in trivia than this. New Jersey seems like the most random of the three, so I write a "b" on our answer sheet.

I look up just as Henry gives Cameron a signal.

"What's going on?" I ask Henry.

"Have I ever told you how amazing you look in yellow?" he asks, kissing me on my neck. He's trying to distract me.

"You're up to something," I reply. "Will this all be roller coaster trivia?"

Henry shrugs. It's totally something he would do.

"Okay," Cameron interrupts from the microphone. "Question number 3: What album did Miley Cyrus's smash hit, 'Party in the USA' appear on? Was it a. *Time of Our Lives*, b. *Bangerz* or c. *Can't Be Tamed*?"

I put my pencil down. This is adorable. It's just like Henry to do something romantic like this.

Henry bolts from his chair and rips the microphone from Cameron's hand.

What is happening? Oh my God, is it...

"I have my own trivia question," Henry says in the microphone. My heart stops.

"Will she say yes?" Henry asks as he signals to Cameron. "Hit it."

The opening chords of "Party in the USA" begin, and Henry grabs my hands and nestles his lips in my hair.

"Baby, I have something to ask you," he says. I'm sobbing as he pulls me to the middle of the open area. I don't know what to do so I dab my cheeks with my sweat wristbands.

"Raegan Claire Stewart," Henry says, kneeling down to one knee and pulling out a ring box. He opens the hinged lid to show a stunning diamond, and I cover my face with my hands. "will you do me the honor of being my wife?"

I nod, and Henry stands up and drops the mic, causing a terrible sound and a scrambling Cameron. Henry slips the ring on my finger and takes me into his arms.

I'm so in love with this man. It doesn't matter we've been together for only three months. He's my forever.

"I love you," Henry says, kissing me.

"I love you too," I say.

"I invited some people," he says, pointing to the door. Standing in the corner are my parents and Erin and Cassie. I run to them, and we group-hug with tiny hops on the balls of our feet. They pull my hand each direction to look at the ring.

"Aren't you glad I forced you on that date?" Erin asks.

"So happy," I say. "Thank you for making me."

"No problem," Erin says, pulling me in for a hug.

"Look at us," Cassie says. "She met her fiancé on an airplane"—she points at Erin—"I reconnected with Smith in an elevator, and Henry worked his magic when the roller coaster got stuck."

"Dare I say it was fate?" I ask.

"It's something," Erin says. "It's a little weird, actually."

"I'm not mad about it," Cassie says.

"Thank you for coming," I say, hugging them again.

"We wouldn't miss it for the world," Cassie replies. I leave them to hug everyone in the room, including Cameron, but the last person I hug is Henry.

"I guess you're stuck with me now," he says, looping his arms around my waist.

"Always and forever," I reply, kissing him again, so happy to have found my person. All because we got stuck on a roller coaster. Now I'm stuck in love.

THE END

BONUS: WHEN RAEGAN LEFT

HENRY

After she goes into the restaurant, I sit an embarrassingly long time in that parking lot.

Raegan left my arms, and they now feel empty at my sides.

Fearing she'll come out with her friends, laughing and hugging and see me in the parking lot, I turn my car on and whip out of the driveway to blaring horns.

I barely hear them as I head back to my condo, lost in a daze.

My time with Raegan feels like a dream, something I would wake up from with a smile on my face. I knew she didn't like me when we met at Thrill Mountain yesterday and my nerves didn't help. Ironically, it took one stuck roller coaster for me to relax and then she got to know me.

The real me.

I usually don't break out the dance moves for at least seven months.

When I get back to my apartment, I drop the keys with a clang on my counter. My gaze hits my bed, where we had a magical night last night, full of passion and intense eye contact. I could have never planned for Raegan.

Not at all.

Usually, I'd turn on the TV or my speakers for some sound, because silence is too loud sometimes. But, if I do, it'll distract me from memorizing every detail of her, how she felt in my arms, how her skin felt under my fingertips.

I said, *I just wish things were different* and I meant that.

Long distance relationships don't work. One summer where I went home to Healdsburg while my college girl-friend stayed in Boston, she cheated on me because she was lonely. *We were never meant to be*, she said after she confessed and I spent the rest of the summer wandering up and down our small-town streets, wondering if I should've stayed.

Time told me that even proximity wouldn't have held us together. Proximity makes lots of people feel like they found the one.

I can't believe I so quickly dismissed Raegan. Semi-retired, I have lots of flexibility and there's many companies who would let me work remote and pay me to do it. I love San Francisco but the city has changed, more than I'd ever like to admit. I've been to Raegan's hometown Goldheart once and it's charming and small, a popular tourist lake town. It did remind me of home and that's why I liked it so much.

However, maybe my presence would remind Raegan of a life she wished she could live. San Francisco is in her bones and she's tearing herself away to get her head right. Finally make the adult decisions. All I make is adult decisions. This condo, for instance. My mom suggested it and I signed on the dotted line, but it feels more like an anchor than wings.

Raegan's free spirit made me dance, made me stand up

to a disruptive couple on the roller coaster. I pushed her against a wall, something I've never done, because I needed her lips on mine.

My fingertips go to my lips instinctually and I remember how it felt.

It wasn't there with my last girlfriend, what everyone looks for.

Magic.

Aimless for hours, my stomach finally reminds me I am here. Without a thought, I flick open the DoorDash app and find my last order and order it again. It's a surprise that it's a giant burrito from my favorite place in the Mission district.

I barely taste it as I chew.

"You've looked better," Landon says when I open the door. Rubbing my face, I take a quick glance at the mirror. Deep, blue circles under my eyes, reddish scruff along my chin. He's right.

"I haven't been sleeping." I rub my eyes, but it doesn't work.

"Erin said that you and Raegan hit it off."

"We did."

"Also said you dropped her off at brunch and she was wearing the same clothes."

"I can neither confirm nor deny. I'm a gentleman." I smack my hand over my chest.

"Uh huh." He walks to my couch and opens his laptop for our brainstorming session. Landon has been itching for a new project, but my head feels heavy, and this apartment has been my prison for the last five days. My best friend looks around the space and notices the empty containers and the clothes piling on the floor.

"You're usually cleaner than this. You also haven't made a joke yet. Are you okay?"

"Define okay."

"You're wearing your Depression Crocs."

I look down although I know my feet are encased in glorified Styrofoam. Out of habit, I click them together at the heels. Landon grimaces.

"God, they're ugly." He grabs his phone and starts tapping buttons.

"What are you doing?"

"Texting Erin. She needs to be here."

"Why?"

Landon holds his phone and then a dial tone sounds from it. Waving my hands, I lunge at the phone. "No, no, no..."

"Hello?" Erin's voice drifts from the phone. Silently, I open my mouth to scream at Landon.

"Hey, I'm here with Henry. You're on speaker."

"Hi Henry." Erin's voice sounds like I did something wrong. Like Raegan told her I did something wrong. Uh-oh. I clench my butt cheeks, waiting for the boom to lower.

"So, I'm at Henry's condo. It's *dirty* in here and he's wearing his Crocs."

"Oh no." She sounds concerned. So what if Crocs make me feel better and I don't feel like cleaning up although I usually keep this place spic and span?

"Can you tell Henry what you told me after you got home from brunch last weekend?"

"Oh, um, Henry, Raegan cried *the whole time*."

My face spreads to a stupid grin. "Really?"

"You should see his face, babe. Henry, I can't believe you." Landon's expression is stone until it breaks into a grin.

"Is he smiling?"

"Yes. Big time."

"I just had a really nice time with Raegan," I admit.

"Then, riddle me this Batman. Why did you tell her you couldn't talk or see where things go? Goldheart isn't that far from San Francisco."

"It's just...she's finding herself, you know."

"Henry, my lovely Henry." Erin pauses and I know she's going to eviscerate me. "I need any reason to get Raegan to stay here. She's going to be *miserable* in that tiny town. We offered her my couch until she gets on her feet. You need to tell her so I can get her back. I'm selfish."

"Really, man, Erin wanted me to kidnap Raegan so she couldn't leave." Landon looks up.

"She was really smitten with you."

"She was?" I light up even more and step out of the Crocs.

"He's taking the Crocs off, babe," Landon tells the phone.

"I think you like her too, Henry. You're just scared."

Everything about her has consumed my thoughts. The events of our date and stuck roller coaster flash through my mind like a movie. It sounds crazy but that date is how I imagined meeting my wife would be like. Holy shit, am I thinking like that?

"I do like her. A lot." I pause. "What if it doesn't work out? Because of the distance?"

"Henry, I feel this with every fiber of my being. If you start dating and it goes the way I think it's going to, she'll be back in town before you know it. She's not a small-town girl. She's a dirty, frigid city girl who got pickpocketed twice in Paris and insisted it was her fault. Urban is in her blood. Let's get her back."

"So, what'll it be, Stallion? You gonna get her?"

My feet scurry across my condo as my thoughts bounce from one scenario to the next. I can't help it; I bite my thumb nail. If I don't go after her, I'll spend the rest of my life wondering what if. I've only felt the magic I've been looking for once. It's what I felt while I was on a stuck roller coaster and then over a churro and then over a corn dog.

The decision is easy.

"I guess, I have to go get her."

The next day, I'm in my car, gassed up, with a bouquet of green, blue, and pink flowers in a vase with water sitting in my passenger seat. When I went to my local florist, I saw the bouquet, off to the side, sad and alone. It was the most beautiful bouquet to me, though. It reminded me of Raegan's hair.

Miley Cyrus is on a loop and when "Party in the USA" comes on, I accidentally start speeding and slow down in time when I see a California Highway Patrol officer in the distance.

I drive through Sacramento and then head east, into rolling hills and winding roads until I hit the town limits of Goldheart. It's exactly as I remember—a relic of a bygone's time, with a lot of the original building from the Gold Rush boom. I slow to a crawl, scanning the area for a woman who matches the flowers next to me.

Erin gave me her family's address, but I assume she'll be out and about and not at home. My last resort will be showing up at her door.

I park my car in an angled spot next to a park with a white gazebo.

It takes me a little bit of scanning to find her. And there she is.

Her hair's many colors reflecting the sun. That creamy skin I couldn't get enough of.

Seeing her again confirms everything I felt. My stomach is in knots. My heart pounds. It feels like I'm stepping into the next phase of my life where the what- if is answered.

Even if I'm destroyed, even if she feels differently now that she's had distance, at least I will know.

I see a tall red-haired woman, walking next to her. That must be her sister. Nervousness rushes through my veins. It's now or never.

I hope she'll be happy to see me.

I don't know though because everything about this feels right. In my bones, it feels like I'm walking to my future wife.

I take a deep breath, grab the flowers, still dripping water from the stems and take a step forward towards the woman that changed my world a week ago.

WANT MORE?

Thank you so much for reading! If you enjoyed this trilogy, please review on Amazon and tell the other readers in your life about this collection. It would mean so much!

Erin, Cassie, and Sarah first appeared in *Here*, the first book in my *Here in Lillyvale* series. They're hype girls for my main character Zoey in the bathroom.

Annie, Raegan's older sister, has a book! *Fool's Gold*, the first book in my Finch Family series is available now, in ebook and paperback.

To stay in touch with me, please join my newsletter! Go to my website, jennybuntingbooks.com, to subscribe.

ABOUT THE AUTHOR

Jenny Bunting started writing stories as a kid, and romance has always been her favorite. She "published" books by designing construction paper covers and still has a horde of them to this day. Jenny has had over thirty jobs, including working at a newspaper, at the mall, as a substitute teacher, and currently works a government job. She loves peanut butter, puns, exercise, reading, brunch, and IPAs. Jenny lives with her husband and German shepherd in the suburbs of Sacramento, California.

www.ingramcontent.com/pod-product-compliance
Lightning Source LLC
Chambersburg PA
CBHW060909250626
47159CB00008B/2934